In memory of my father William Fraley, who taught us kids nothing is too far out of reach if you work hard enough for it. Rest In Peace.

THE POWERS THAT BE

Paul Fraley

AuthorHouse™
1663 Liberty Drive
Bloomington, IN 47403
www.authorhouse.com
Phone: 1 (800) 839-8640

Published by AuthorHouse 07/09/2018

ISBN: 978-1-5462-4353-3 (sc)
ISBN: 978-1-5462-4354-0 (e)

Library of Congress Control Number: 2018906163

Print information available on the last page.

This book is printed on acid-free paper.

authorHOUSE®

The powers that be - A Scifi adventure in comedy (trilogy).

ACT - 1. THE POWER UNLEASHED.

Chapter One

Mike Ferral had just finished a busy day selling shoes at the shoe store where he worked and had just come home from a hard day's work, his brother inlaw's stationwagon was sitting in the driveway parked on the right side. It was starting to rain and Mike had a strong urge to use the bathroom, he stepped inside the door and shivered, then looked about as he walked into the kitchen, "Hello, anybody here", he queried. Then deciding that he couldn't wait for a reply to his question he pushed the bathroom door open after he knocked on it twice, and stepped inside and shed his jacket and flung it into the empty tub, and closed, and locked the door behind him.

Then unbuttoning his pants and pulling down his longjohns after grabbing a towel, he then raised the lid to the toilet and sat down. After drying off his head from the rain he draped the towel over his lap and started to grunt. As if by Magic, it was as if a giant shadow from overhead suddenly covered the room then, there were thousands of twinkling stars in front of him where the tub had been, he was on the toilet surrounded by pitch blackness and millions of twinkling stars on all sides as far as the eye could see. Suddenly, off to his right there was a bright yellow circle, only it had a face, it was a smiley face! "Well, my goodness" exclaimed the smiley face, "That certainly is an odd looking vehicle, ah yes I seem to recall its make now, almost obsolete you know" he said to Mike in his British accent.

"Who the devil, or what are you!?" Exclaimed Mike. "I sir" said the smiley face, "am part navigator, part Scientist, and to boot I have an infinite amount of toilet paper hidden on my person" rattled off the smiley face.

"I am here to provide guidance" went on the smiley face, "to you sir, so that you may travel anywhere in the universe so long as you sit on that toilet and use it." The smiley face spoke in a very high pitched voice with a thick British accent- "Call me Bob" said the smiley face, " I am of the race of Astral beamers who patrol the highways and byways of Outer Space, the reason we smiley faces all smile so much comes from the fact that we all have access to so much toilet paper." Meanwhile Erik Macintosh found himself buzzing someone's apartment door. To his Amazement his wife Judith appears at the door and she is totally naked. "Hello Erik" she giggled, "come on in, join the party" said Judith. She stepped aside and pulled Erik halfway through the door, "We're fixing dinner, we're having chicken", she giggled again, "What's the matter Erik, you're not chicken are you?" She pulled him the rest of the way into the apartment and shut the door behind

him. "What's going on here Judith," he demanded angrily. "Oh poo, just settle down and I will introduce you to Sadie and Lucy, they're helping with dinner" she replied. The two other naked women entered the hall and sauntered into the living room in front of Erik, they looked like they were in their late twenties or early thirties. "I'm Lucy" said one of the attractive nude women, "Lucy Spaneli." "Who's this handsome male" chimed in Sadie, "Do we have a dinner guest this evening? I hope he likes chicken."

"And That's Sadie" said Lucy, "She turns tricks." "Tricks? Oh what a shame I didn't bring any cards" replied Erik. Sadie Smiled and said, "Sayy, that's clever, wish I thought of that." Erik looked back at Judith, "Do you have any idea how bad this looks?" He Whispered quite loudly, then he said "I am getting a headache." "Poor dear", said Judith, "Why don't you go into the bedroom and lie down for a while, I promise to save you a breast", the corner of her mouth turned up at saying that and formed a crooked smile, "Oh I'm sorry you're probably a leg man", and with that she walked across the room and stood in front of a door. "Judith", He spoke in a low voice, "don't you realize what this looks like?" "Yes" she retorted quite loudly, "By the way Erik, did I mention I'm Bi, as in bisexual, maybe this will take care of your headache dear", and with that she swung the door behind her open wide and shoved Erik inside, she closed the door behind him and said-"Enjoy". In the dimly lit room sat a light brown haired girl on the edge of the bed facing him, she wore a low cut red miniskirt with black stalkings and her shoes high heel pink pumps. At first he didn't quite get it, not until he took a few steps forward and took a long look at her, it was Candace Tameron the actress. "Hey, you're that young girl from TV, I know you"…

"You will discover that here there are different rules" she said, "First of all my friend, you will call me TJ and I will call you Paul, come lay next to me on this bed so that our fluids may mingle and become one", she licked her ruby red lips, "I want you" she said. When she grinned she exposed two pointy fangs in plain view and her eyes of red fire glowed eerily at him, "What's wrong lover", she stood up a foot or so away from the bed, "Don't you believe in Vampires?" By now Erik was shaking with fear, visibly so, and he stuttered when he tried to speak- "I, I, I, I, I, I Buhb, buh, buh, buh, buh, believe in Vampires……." Replied Erik. Suddenly she sprang forward and lunged at him and clenched his trenchcoat tightly in her hands, she growled fiercely "I'm hungry Paul, you must feed me, I cant wait to sink my fangs into some fresh meat!!" Erik stuttered, "Frr, f, f, f, fresh, sh, me, me, me, me, meat….? You muh, me, me, me, mean chic, chic, chic, chicken!"She tore his trench coat off of him, "Warm blood is what I want human!" "Whoa!" said Erik, "Now I know what must have happened to Paul!!"

Gaining courage Erik makes the sign of the cross by crossing the index "fingers of each hand, "Back Hellspawn" he stopped shaking with fear, faith on his side, "Return to your bed of sin"! She shrieked as if in pain but ran back to the bed. The sun is in my image, the rays of the Morning are filling this room, sleep Vampire, Sleep, go to sleep…..", replied Erik. She lay back on the bed and closed her eyes, "Paul" she whispered and fell fast asleep. Tip toeing Erik bends down to pick up his trench coat, standing there, then blows Candace a kiss and whispers "Candace Tameron lying on a bed and I'm leaving without a kiss, sounds like a bad dream; I always liked her."

Then tip toeing he quietly opened the door and walked through it and carefully closed it behind him as quietly as possible, "Sh- Vampire sleeping" he whispered. All three women are standing around wearing house robes as if they all had simultaneously stepped out of the shower, Judith was busy munching on a drum stick, Sadie was puffing on a cigarette and Lucy was standing there blowing the nail polish on her nails.

"Hey girls", Erik whispered "Where's the Can,I gotta go do number two." Lucy volunteered by slowly walking across the room, " Follow me Chief, its

this way", said Lucy. He followed her into the Hallway up to a doorway on the left, "The light switch is on the wall to the right" she said, and left him there. Quickly figuring out where the light switch was Erik flipped it on and then gently shut the door behind him. The next sensation is a bit difficult to describe, one minute the toilet, shower and bath, the sink and closet, were all there and then for about a second gray fog surrounded him on all sides and then the next moment Erik was standing in the middle of some kind of laboratory. In front of him about five feet away was a strange looking table and strapped to it was a Pale man in dark clothing, his forehead and wrists had hideous stitches. Suddenly from behind someone cleared their throat- "Ahem!" Erik whirled around and looked to see a small flight of three stairs and an upraised floor upon which stood a red haired man wearing a white lab coat. The man cleared his throat once more and spoke, "I am Dr. Frankenstein, Victor Frankenstein, you are Erik Macintosh I take it??"

"Yeah, but that doesn't explain why Im here" retorted Erik.

Dr. Frankwinner descended the steps, "That young man should be quite obvious! You shall assist me, in bringing my creation to life!!"

"Say Doc, has anyone ever told you that you look exactly like Donald Cartridge?" The Doctor smiled and said, "Yeah, I get that a lot." Dr. Frankwinner stepped forward and held out to Erik what looked like a twelve inch long Marijuana cigarette, Erik took it and Dr. Frankwinner whipped out another and stuck it in his mouth and lit it, "Don't worry Erik its Just Marijuana, it has a medicinal use for my creature", said Dr. Frankwinner. Erik stuck an end to his mouth and Dr. Frankwinner took his bic Lighter and lit it for him- "You stand close on this side of his head" said Dr. Frankwinner "And I will stand on the opposite side of his head, we will puff on the cigarettes, um, er, doobies, and blow smoke into his ears, understand? Yah, good boy!" Then the good Doctor did as he said, he walked around the head of the table and stood on the opposite side of the table puffing on his joint. Erik stopped puffing, "Say Doc, I really hate to bring this up but Frankenstein is a Fictional character created by Mary Shelly." "That's because you're dreaming Erik, and you have to do number two!" Shouted Doctor Frankenstein. "Come again", Said Erik "What did you say?" "I said you have to Shit!" Shouted Dr. Frankwinner, then began his maniacal laughter, very evil sounding. "Ha, Ha, Ha,Ha, Haa!" Thunder clapped, he said it again- "You have to shit!" The last word echoed loudly, "Shit-Shit-it-it!" Erik awoke on the couch in Mike Ferral's living room, "God, what a nightmare!" Exclaimed Erik,

"Oh no, I gotta go take a shit!" Erik leaped off the couch and ran to the bathroom door and began pounding on the door. "Mike, I have to have the toilet, Mike I gotta Shit! Mike!" Yelled Erik as he pounded on the door. Meanwhile back at the magic toilet, things were quite different……

Mike Sat on his toilet which floated about in deep space, and stared at the smiley face which spoke to him. "As I was Saying said the Astral beamer, I'm your Astral beamer, I will look out for you whenever you sit on the Johnny Stool" he said in a thick British accent, " And don't worry the Magick in the toilet works only for you Mike, we're going to have many adventures together……don't be frightened Mike, I'm here to see you don't get lost! By the way, want some toilet paper?" Asked the Astral beamer.

"How do I get back home", asked Mike. "Oh, that's easy, just jiggle the handle three times, then flush good and hard and presto, you're there", said Bob, "To find me just put your naked bum against the toilet seat and grunt once, and that's that!" Exclaimed Bob the Astral beamer. Mike jiggled the handle three times and flushed, good and hard. Suddenly the black star studded expanse of space was replaced by his own bathroom once more. Thump, Thump, Thump, his brother inlaw was beating at the door. "Mike, I gotta Shit, hurry up and get out!" Mike wiped his bum and pulled up his longjohns and his pants, and washed his hands. " Just keep yer shirt on, I'm hurrying, I'm hurrying", he said as he was drying his hands on a towel. He grabbed his jacket then he unslid the bolt on the bathroom door, and opened it. "Say Mike, anybody ever tell you that you look exactly like Al Grundy?" asked Erik. "Yeah, I get that a lot", said Mike.

Chapter Two

The next day Mike called in sick, it was 9 AM and Mike was craving that first cup of coffee. He slowly roused himself from his bed where he sat after talking on the phone. He shuffled into the kitchen and went for the instant coffee, he took it from the cabinet and set it on the table, then he searched for his favorite mug and found it, he filled it up with water from the kitchen tap and walked over to the microwave oven and put his mug of water in it and set the controls for two and a half minutes, and pushed the start button. He stood there hypnotically transfixed to that spot in front of the microwave just staring at the numbers as they counted down and the microwave made its familiar hum. then before you knew it-"Beeeeep" chimed the microwave, he opened the door and took his mug in hand and set it on the table, whereupon setting it down he turned back to the cabinet to fetch a spoon, a teaspoon to be exact. So upon fetching the spoon he then opened the jar of instant coffee and scooped up one teaspoon of it and dumped it into the mug of hot water, as he stood there stirring his mug of coffee he reflected on his impossible screwy experience of the other day. Had it actually happened? In a way it all seemed like a crazy dream but at the same time on some level of his mind he considered it to be very real, it took all the self control he had to keep from blurting out everything that had happened to him, to his brother in law, but the thought had occurred to him- "What if he thinks I've gone insane?" And so he kept silent about it. After putting a generous amount of milk and sugar into his coffee he shuffled back to his bedroom while his coffee cooled on the table.

He dressed himself Quickly and then returned to the kitchen for his mug of coffee, he pulled out a chair from the table and lifted his mug as he sat down and blew across the top of his mug to cool the coffee, then sitting down he sipped it and just stared into space, then thought outloud "Got to find out if last night was actually real." It took fifteen minutes to drink that cup of coffee but he had managed to do it and then stood up from the table, "and now, its time" said Mike, he walked over to the bathroom door slowly, then upon reaching it he opened the bathroom door.

"No time like the present" he said, then he entered the room and shut the door behind him and out of force of habit he locked the door, and then he went through the routine of raising the lid and pulled down his pants and upon sitting down urinated in the Toilet while waiting for the fun to begin.

One minute he was doing his business, the next minute the wind started blowing through the room from out of nowhere, as if a big fan had been turned on. Suddenly the room was replaced by an expanse of blue sky, the sun was behind him and there were instantly clouds drifting by his toilet.

Meanwhile aboard the 747 jet airliner that was rapidly coming up on him, a discovery of sorts was about to take place. The Copilot said to the pilot "Captain do you see that? What can it be?" A tiny man on a tiny toilet darted about slightly above the cloud level. The pilot picked up the radio microphone, "Uh-Control tower we'd like to report a U.F.O." Said the pilot. Suddenly something brown flew out of the bottom of the toilet and was flying straight at the plane. "Captain, it's fired something at us, it's coming right at us" said the Copilot. The Windshield was suddenly splattered with brown feces, a big smear of poop covered one entire side of the forward windshield, "Sir" said the Copilot, "I think you should know that there is Shit on our windshield" reported the Copilot to the Pilot. The Pilot continued to communicate with the ground, "Control tower, disregard my last statement, its just some birdshit on our windshield."

Back at the toilet, the smiley face had just recently manifested itself to Mike. "No, No, No, never jiggle the handle only once before flushing, that way it fires missles of crap! You should have waited and asked me about it first" remarked Bob the Smiley face. "Say, Smiley, what keeps me from falling if I stand up?"Asked Mike. "Oh that's easy, the toilet is surrounded by a technospacial force field, which is why the stars seem to twinkle from photon distortion when it's in deep space, but if you stand there for more than two minutes it will shut off and you would then fall to your death, by the way I prefer if you call me Bob", said Bob. "Yeah thanks Bob, that's all good stuff to know," replied Mike. Mike then jiggled the handle three times waited for about a minute and then flushed good and hard but to his surprise a fog horn sounded and multicolored lights suddenly swirled around the toilet and then Mike felt the toilet fall, he gripped the bowl of the toilet tightly and screamed for awhile as the toilet fell out of the sky. "Bob, what did I do, what's going on here!!??"Asked Mike, but the smiley face was gone and was no where to be seen. Finally the toilet slowed down and slowly touched down on the ground with a thump just outside of a strange looking building. "Bob?" Mike looked around, suddenly there was a popping sound and the smiley face was suddenly hovering about five feet off the ground. "Boy am I glad I finally caught up to you, Mike you shouldn't have hesitated after jiggling three times, this time when you flushed you wound up in a parallel universe! Now you have to wait a few hours before returning home." Replied Bob. " What do you suggest I do Bob?" asked Mike, "Well, we could start by having a look around" said Bob. After pulling up his pants Mike walked around for about an hour with the smiley face hovering around following behind him, mostly there were just trees and bushes, and then suddenly there was the sound of rushing water, splashing and laughing. A few feet away through a tall bush Mike could see a river with people swimming around in it, suddenly a girl who had been treading water began to scream for help, she flailed around wildly. It was apparent to Mike that she was too tired to tread water anymore, many people in loincloths or white robes stood around on the bank while the girl cried for help, but they did absolutely nothing but stand there. "Oh my," said Bob as he was trying to get a closer look, "what seems to be the matter here??"Mike stepped into the clearing and yelled, "Somebody do something, save her!" The bystanders just stared at him or at the girl and did nothing as the girl flailed wildly and screamed. Mike, getting frustrated, then dove in after the girl and putting an arm around her and using the other arm to stroke the water, swam back to the bank with girl in tow beside him. Then holding her hand with his he hoisted her up onto the bank and held her for a moment in his arms, "Are you alright" he asked. "I'm fine" she said. "Bravo Master Mike" bellowed Bob the Astral beamer, "Good show!" The girl looked into Mike's face and said "Why did you help me?" "Don't be silly" said Mike "You needed helping So I helped you." "What's that?" She said as she pointed at Bob who had just happened to be hovering behind Mike's shoulder. "What's that? Oh, that's just Bob. He's okay" said Mike.

"My name is Mina" said the girl, "how are you called, what is your name?" "My name is Mike Ferral, you can call me Mike", said Mike. "Come with me, I will show you where to find food" said Mina. They walked for about half an hour when Mike looked up at what was apparently a city, a city without traffic. "What are your people called Mina?" asked Mike, "We are called Soloi" she said. They walked into a courtyard of sorts with Bob floating along beside them, there were many tables set out laden with fruits and vegetables, and many people sat at the tables and feasted. Mina and Mike sat down at the table next to an incredibly fat young man who was eating red grapes. Bob hovered above some light green grapes on the table and put out his yellow hands which were invisible before and started to sample the green grapes, "mmm, this is pretty good stuff" said Bob. Quite Abruptly a flatuating noise began, it seemed as if the fat man was breaking wind, quite loudly too. Mike made an ugly face "oooooh that's disgusting, cut that out and get out of here!" Mike shouted at the fat man. "I've never been so disgusted in all my life!" Said Mike.

The fat man just looked up at them as if to say-Who me? But said nothing and only got up to leave but as soon as he did the sound began again, but instead of seeing someone farting as Mike fully expected, instead there was a thin young man in white robes with a bare arm exposed to his mouth making that rude noise with his arm pressed against his mouth. Upon seeing Mike's mean glare, he stopped doing it and started to laugh and kept laughing as he got up and walked away. Mike then sampled a Banana, "Where are your records, your libraries Mina, do you or your people have books?" "Yes", she said, "We have books,

but no one knows how to read them, once a long time ago our people knew how to read but we have forgotten how" said Mina.

"Where is this place, this Library, can you take me there?" Asked Mike, "it's this big building next to the courtyard" she pointed. " can you show me mina?" Asked Mike, "Yes, come with me and I will show you, it will be dark soon and it is best that we be behind locked doors before the Woelocks come" said Mina. "The Woelocks? Who are they" asked Mike. "Providers, but it is said that they are ugly and only come out at night" said Mina, "Come". They walked into the building, Bob floated in behind them, Mina locked the door behind them, "The books are up those stairs and to the right" said Mina. They went up the stairs and into the room, a room with many shelves of books and a white and silver cabinet. "Here we may consult with computer" said Mina, "A computer?" said Mike, "Where?" Mina walked up to the cabinet and pushed a small blue stud and lights flashed on and off in the wall. "Computer working" said the wall. "Where do you get your power, computer?" asked mike, "Solar Power cells on roof of this building and main power battery, this unit is programmed to function no longer than five minutes without having questions put to it to save power", said the wall. "What happened to this civilization and who are the Woelocks?" Asked Mike. "After the Neutron bomb was detonated, underground sanctuaries were built, a mutant gene threatened Society, it was called Sasquatch syndrome, the educational system broke down and the Woelocks who were mutated dominated the local economy as well as agriculture and industry. The Woelocks prefer dimly lit areas because that is the state of technology underground, the Woelocks need the Soloi people for breeding material. Soloi are dependant upon Woelocks whose appearance is humanoid but covered in hair or fur", finished the wall, and then it was silent. "Well" said Mike "Let's not run down his batteries, if it's getting dark we should look for a place to sleep." "There is another room, through that doorway and up two flights of stairs there should be a bedroom, it used to be the caretaker's room" said Mina. They went up the two flights of stairs and found a bedroom, it was spacious with blue carpet and paneled walls, the bed was a king sized bed. Mina sat on one side of the bed, Bob floated down at the foot of the bed and touched down on the bed, " I guess I'll take the foot of the bed" said Bob, "We leave first thing tomorrow" said Mike. They each laid down on the bed fully clothed and went to sleep.

Chapter Three

Meanwhile back on earth at Erik and Judith Macintosh's house Erik and his wife slept in their bedroom and Erik dreamed. Erik dreamed of a blue sky and a blue ocean underneath it, and of an aircraft carrier the size of a Volkswagon. He was stark naked, spreadeagled face down on the deck of the miniature ship. Something by Pink Floyd was playing in the background, it was "Us and Them" from the Dark Side of the Moon album. He grunted as if in pain, then he grunted some more as if he was trying to fart. At first only the head of the Baby Whale was visible coming from out of his anus, "ohhhhh Baby this is a long one, C'mon Skippy you can do it boy!!" Shouted Erik as he grunted once more. Now all but the tail was outside of Erik's anus, "Oh God, it's a big one!!" Shouted Erik, and he grunted once more for a long time. Now the tail was out and the whale was making human infant noises, it was crying. Then Erik got up and crouched down bending over the Baby whale and picked it up in his arms and tossed it into the water. "C'mon, fly boy. You can do it Skippy, c'mon I believe in you!" Yelled Erik. Suddenly the Whale leaped up out of the water and sprouted Butterfly wings and flew away high up in the sky. Then suddenly Erik was dressed in a green shiny metallic suit (similar to the kind Ellen Degeneres likes to wear, Ha Ha:) and he was standing on top of a flying saucer which was hovering above his home. Then the next second after that he was in his bedroom staring at a woman with short brown hair who looked suspiciously like Lori Loughlin, and who just happened to also have on a green metallic suit, and she had a thick moustache glued to her upper lip. "Human" She said "I am of the Galaxian race, you will take this bra and wear it on your head to show that you are a conquered people." "What bra?" Erik said, "This one" replied the alien, she pointed at his head and the next thing he knew, there was a green beam of light shooting out of her finger as the room was filled with the theme music from the TV show the next step beyond, and suddenly there was a bra on his head fastened beneath his chin. "You know you're sexy when you're mad" said Erik, "Is that why I'm always hot and bothered!" Exclaimed the female Alien who looked a heck of a lot like Rebecca from the TV sitcom BullHouse. Then Quite abruptly without warning Erik awoke from his dream to find that his wife Judith was shaking him awake. "Erik" she said "You're dreaming of another woman aren't you? You were talking in your sleep! Who is Skippy, is that the name of your Whore!?" Ranted Judith. "Go back to sleep Judy, I was only dreaming about space aliens, let me get back to sleep! I'm bushed" replied Erik. The next day on the world of the Soloi Mike Ferral was just Starting his day and Mina and Bob were close behind.

Mike walked out into the courtyard with Mina and Bob following him, "C'mon we've got to find my toilet, only a few people are up at this hour, I don't want anyone else messing with my magic toilet" said Mike.

So they walked back to the area where Mike's toilet had landed, but when they arrived at the strange looking building the toilet was gone! Mike looked down at the ground where the toilet had been, there were marks on the ground where something had been dragged across the ground and up to the closed door of the building. "Look here" said Mike, "It looks as if someone dragged my toilet into this building!" he said. Then Suddenly there was a very loud noise filling the air, it was an air raid siren. Strangely enough it seemed to be attracting people, then the door of the building slid open and Mina started to walk into the building. "No!" Shouted Mike "You don't have to breed with them" he grabbed her by the wrist and said "This may be rather sudden Mina, but will you marry me, I'll take you back to my world and teach you how to read!" Yelled Mike above the din of the air raid siren. "Why Yes, I'd love to be your wife Mike!" Mina replied. "Then c'mon guys, we have a toilet to find!" He shouted as he charged through the doorway. Waiting there next to his toilet however was a hairy humanoid thing with bare breasts of a female, it took a step toward Mike and said "Gimmie some sugar Baby."

Mike punched her right in the face and threw her against the wall, then taking his bic lighter out of his pocket he lit it and took Mina by the hand. Then he sat down on the toilet without pulling his pants down because Bob was already there and He sat Mina on his lap. Jiggling the handle three times and then flushing really hard he said "Okay Bob, let's go!!" "Is that another lighter in your pocket Mike or are you just glad to see me? Asked Mina. " I'm Just glad you're aboard Baby, I'm just glad you're aboard!" Said Mike, The next instant two things happened, the bic in Mike's hand grew too hot to hold and he dropped it and Multicolored lights swirled around the toilet as it began to move up and forward through the door way, the next minute they were in the sky and then they felt the toilet drop rapidly and then suddenly before you knew it they were back in Mike's Bathroom safe and sound.

Meanwhile back at Erik and Judith's place Judith was pacing back and forth and Erik was sitting on the couch in the living room playing with a slinky. "I want to find out what that brother inlaw of mine is up to", "what are you doing there playing with that toy?" Asked Judith. "I'm trying to come up with a Jingle for Amigo Condoms Judy, it's for an ad Campaign and I only have Three weeks to come up with something for Fate and McFann", Said Erik. "Well I'm going to call Mike and I think you should go over there and pay him another visit. I called his place of work and they said he was sick or something. Ohhh, what's that number of his…." Said Judith. Judith picked up the phone, then she punched out his number on the phone keys and waited as the phone rang on the other end of the line.

Mike Ferral picked up the phone on the third ring, "Hello, this is Mike. Who am I speaking to?" said Mike. "Mike, this is Judy, I'm just calling to ask how you're doing, I heard that you were sick, what's the deal?" Said Judith. "Oh it's nothing Sis, Just a little headcold, nothing serious. I'm just knocking off a couple days of work, oh I've got good news.

Listen, you'll love this, guess what?" Said Mike. "What" said Judith. "I'm getting married" said Mike, "Married!? Who's the lucky girl?" Asked Judith, "A girl by the name of Mina" replied Mike. "Well congratulations, that's wonderful, listen, if you're not going anywhere in the next two hours, Erik and me are going to drop in on you to say Hello if that's alright," said

Judith. "Sure, sure, swing on by, we'll be here", said Mike. "Okey dokey, see you in a little bit, bye bye", replied Judith. Judith hung up the phone, "Did you hear that Erik, Mike is getting married!!" said Judith, "Do you think he might want some rubbers?" Asked Erik.

Meanwhile back at Mike's place Mike and Mina are kissing and groping each other like mad, when suddenly Mike sees something outside the window out the corner of his eye. "Hold it hun, what the devil is that!?" Mike exclaimed as he looked toward his living room window. Thousands of flying saucers were hovering above the houses in his neighborhood. "We're being invaded!" exclaimed Mike, "I've got to do something before they start to land!" "What are you going to do Mike?" Asked Mina. "Bob will know what to do, I've got to talk to Bob" Mike said excitedly. Mike ran to the bathroom door, "You stay in there on the couch honey, This is a job I have to do alone!"Shouted Mike. He quickly opened the bathroom door and slammed it behind him, forgetting to lock it this time he quickly pulled down his pants and Long Johns and then raised the lid to the toilet and sat down on the toilet seat. He grunted once and then said, "Bob for God's sake, where are ya man!?" Suddenly in the blink of an eye Mike and the toilet were hovering in the sky above his neighborhood just above a flying saucer and Bob was floating there at eye level just off to his right. "Evil Galaxians by the looks of things" said Bob, "I've seen this sort of thing before, they're apparently a race of hair lipped women according to our news reports bent on world conquest of each world they come to" said Bob. "What are we gonna do Bob?" Said Mike in an exasperated tone, "There's only one thing to do" said Bob,

"Hold on Mike!" Suddenly the toilet Mike was sitting on transformed itself into a Phantom Jet fighter with Bob floating next to Mike in the Cockpit, "Here we gooooo!" cried Bob. A Laser beam shot out of the nose of the Jetplane and the plane flew over all of the flying saucers and each time it would pass over one a laser beam lanced out of the nose of the craft and disintegrated a flying saucer. Soon all of the Saucers had been disintegrated, Music from everywhere in the Sky began playing, it was from Pink Floyd's Dark side of the moon album, it was "Eclipse". The song began when the first flying saucer had been disintegrated and it could be heard in mike's Cockpit. When all of the Alien SpaceVehicles had been destroyed the plane did a loop and then a roll, "Every now and then I feel like listening to some tunes" said Bob. The Plane then transformed itself back into a toilet and rematerialized back in Mike's bathroom. No offense Bob, but I've got to get a new toilet" said Mike, but Bob was Nowhere to be seen.

A little later Erik Macintosh was standing in Mike Ferral's driveway wearing a business suit and wearing a Bra on his head. In his hand were a handful of Amigo condoms. Suddenly from nowhere there was music in the background near Mike's house playing quite loudly which reminded one of a car commercial (Because it used the tune from the slinky commercial) but the people singing in the background sung it slightly different. "Amigo Amigo it's Fun for a girl and a boy!" Erik held up the condoms and said "Amigo Condoms, get yours today! Available at most self service Gas stations."

Chapter Four

Meanwhile Strange powers were brewing mischief in New York, power unleashed from….The Outer worlds. Jack Weinberg the drummer of the band for the Coney Ofryen Show was really having a difficult time understanding what his boss Coney Ofryen was talking about. "It will be great Max" said Coney. "Live at the Olive Garden with Coney Ofryen!" Exclaimed Coney, "It will be big, and we will get you a set of drums that look like giant olives and there you'll be banging on the ol olives giving me a drum roll, and then our anouncer Joseph Godard announces over the microphone- Live at the olive garden-CONEY OFRYEN!" Jack frowned slightly and said, "But why Olives, is it an Irish thing?" "Hey green is beautiful babe, that's why I love the Incredible Bulk cause he's so much like me-Strong and Green, Green as in Cash that is! Said Coney as he grinned and then did his evil mad scientist laugh afterwards, "Ha Ha Ha Ha, Ha Ha Ha!" Jack just raised an eyebrow at that and said "I wonder what's taking Labalmy so long in the restroom?" The two men were standing in the Hallway leading to the studio stage area, Coney Scratched his head for a second and said, "Gee, I dunno but he sure has been spending a lot of time with that bear of ours, maybe they were out drinking beer before the show and he had to go really bad!" Conan Knocked on the rest room door, "La Balmy You've been in there for an hour and a half, C'mon save some toilet paper for the rest of us!" Through the locked door he could hear "Uh, yeah, just a minute Im washing my hands! Ahhhh, Oh God I feel so much better."

After Two Minutes the door opened and LaBalmy Nervously started to make his exit and then accidentally dropped a playhouse magazine from under his arm as he started down the hallway. Jack walked over to the dropped Magazine and said, "oh look Coney, Bathroom literature!" Coney rubbed his chin and gestured with his hand raising his index finger, "Actually Jack that would be Lavatory literature since its way too small to fit a bath in", said Coney. "Ah, yeah okay, its just an expression", said Jack as he held up the Playhouse Magazine and looked at it. "So what was he reading anyhow, Popular Science?" Asked Coney. Grinning Jack closed and Folded the Magazine under his arm, "Oh, its just a trade magazine, with lots of parts in it". Jack walked away at a brisk pace, "See you in Twenty Minutes Coney, gotta get ready for show time!" Later on during the Television show the talkshow host Coney Ofryen was talking to his guest Ned Young. "Then one day there came a Calico Cat and that changed everything", said Ned Young, Suddenly The Incredible Bulk charged onto the set in the middle of the show. Startled, Mr. Young got up and ran out the other door of the studio, and the Bulk got up close to Coney and said, "Bulk want you now Coney!" Coney got up and approached the Bulk, Bulk bellowed at Coney, "On your knees silly man!" Coney got down on both of his knees just as Someone dressed up like Frankenstein's Monster waltzed through the studio doors and eating Popcorn out of a Popcorn bag found a front row seat in the studio audience. Bulk undid his fly. The monster laughed and threw pieces of Popcorn in their

direction. "Ooooooh, take off your clothes Coney!" Shouted The Bulk, "But I'm not gay" pleaded Coney. Just then the Monster whipped out a batter spoon and got up out of the audience and gave it to the Bulk and got back in his seat. The Bulk began spanking Coney's bottom with the batter spoon and then Coney said, "Oh yes that turns me on!" Joseph Godard the Announcer took his Polaroid Camera and took Snapshots of the spectacle. The Guy in the director's booth had been in shock and had let his cigarette burn down to his fingers burning his hand, "Go to commercial" he shouted. Jack was staring in disbelief saying, "C'mon I cant believe this is happening, I'm Jewish, I can't be part of this. Meanwhile the Demon Puck grinned from the Director's booth as he hit the sound effect button for the studio audience that cued a recording of a musical artist singing–"Suck that, suck that!"

The End?…..

ACT - 2. A CLEAN SWEEP.

Chapter One

"So What's The problem!?"Erik Snapped back on the phone, "Teenagers love my ad idea!" "But now people think we're encouraging teenagers under the age of eighteen to have promiscuous Sex,Macintosh, and therefore consumers are now associating Amigo condoms with Child molesters and that's why the account was taken away from us and goodbye to any future Condom accounts because it's too risky to use our services, sorry Erik we have to let you go!" Said the voice at the other end of the line, "Wait Mr. Stephens, we can reshoot the commercial without the eighteen year old twin girls, Please I know this can work" Pleaded Erik, "Click" went the phone and then there was a busy signal. "You can't do this to me, I'm what makes this company great! Mr.Stephens, Mr. Stephenzzzzz, No he hung up on me!" Shouted Erik at the ceiling. "Where did I leave the Paper Judith, I saw a copy of the town crier on the kitchen table this morning, I need the classifieds! I know you were reading Dear Eloweise!" said Erik as he got up from his seat, on his second step he tripped over what seemed to be a rather old model of vacuum sweeper. "Ffuh-youch!" Exclaimed Erik as he banged his elbow on his way down to the floor. "Arhg, my- nose! Did anyone catch the license number on that, that, antique vacuum sweeper?"asked Erik. Judith came walking from the direction of their bedroom with paper in hand, "oh dear, what happened? Did you get that ugly old vac from a garage sale honey? Really, you men are always leaving your clutter where ever you please, never thinking of the consequences!" Erik sat up in the floor on his knees, "Ssssay What, whuh whuh whuh whoa, me, garage sale?" "Wait a minute, this is something your nutty foot fungi salesman brother dragged in here no doubt, unless by some mysterious circumstance I hit my head last night on my pillow got a cuncussion and ran out in the middle of the night in my PeeJays to purchase this monstrosity from an all night garage sale somewhere in our neighborhood,coming back to bed to awake this morning with amnesia! Not only do I have to worry about getting a new job but I have to be on the lookout for mysterious junkpiles in our living room- attacking me!" Judith walked over to Erik, rolled up the newspaper and smacked Erik over the head with it and dropped the paper on the floor in front of him, "Someone woke up with a case of smart ass this morning I see, I can't wait to see what else you dream up, maybe that piece of junk will come to life and bite you on the ass!" She said as she stomped her way to the bathroom. At that moment the vacuum sweeper came roaring to life and the hose of it's own accord attatched itself to Erik's butt and ripped his wallet out of his pants and then shut itself off. Slowly standing up Erik thought out loud in a soft voice, "What just happened here?" Erik checked the wall outlet to see if the vac was plugged in, it wasn't, it was wrapped around the end of the vac, he bent down to pick up the paper facing away from the vacuum cleaner, out of nowhwere a mechanized voice as if from a synthasizer spoke up, "Loser." Standing and unrolling the paper to fold it and tuck it under his arm he sad, "Man that is so annoying when cars drive by the house with their windows down and their boom box radios cranked up fullblast!" He walked in the kitchen and grabbed a pen from the cup sitting on top the refrigerator and sat down looking through the classifieds for a job. " Here's something" he said circling an ad, " Cable serviceman, no experience necessary, on job training." He muttered under his breath, then wanting a piece of toast as his wife walked in with vacuum in hand he opened a loaf of bread. "Forget something?" Judith said before waltzing off to the living room to turn on the television to watch her soaps on daytime TV. Erik went to the fridge to get a tub of butter, sat it on the kitchen table and started to open the lid on the tub of butter, that same mechanized voice spoke up, "Butter", startled he dropped the tub on the table and looked around. "Huh, what?" slowly he picked the tub of butter up and removed the lid, the voice spoke again, "Barrrkayyyy!" Erik's gaze drifted toward the Vacuum in the kitchen floor.

"Nahh, couldn't be" he thought out loud, with paper in hand he went outside and jumped in his car only to find that the car was out of gas, looking at the paper again he said, " six blocks, that's not so far away", so he took to jogging down the road with paper in hand till he found the Cable company office where he put his application in after waiting ten minutes. Then he walked out the office door with a happy tune in his head and started whisteling the tune "if I only had a brain" from the Wizard of Oz as he walked down the street. "Damn" thought Erik, " I really have to go to the bathroom", he looked down the street and spotted O'Mally's bar. He picked up his pace and walked across the street at the corner barbershop and walked into the bar. The cool air from the fan at the bar hit him in the face and felt good, the parrot in the cage behind the bar let out a squawk and said,

"Follow the yellow brick road". "Cute, you'd be perfect for a tire commercial" said Eric, "hey pal" said Erik as he slid a five dollar bill across the bar " can I use your restroom?" "yeah sure, upstairs, take two rights, third door on the left, it aint much but it's all we got." "Thanks Jack" said Erik, "It's Carl, if you can slide me a twenty I can start you a tab" Erik tossed him a twenty," you're a real humanitarian Carl." Erik went up the stairs, the parrot squawked and said "I wanna see the warden, let me outta this cage", "no can do polly, the last time you got out you flew through that hole in the ceiling above the fan, this time no surprises, no mess!" Erik was on the next floor by now and was thinking out loud "that guy said the door on the right, right?

God I've gotta go, I'm gonna crap my pants." He opened the door and walked in and hit the light switch, and saw he was in a utility closet and there was a hole in the floor about the size of a large coffee can. "You've got to be kidding me, I, Uhn no I'm gonna shit my drawers, okay, okay, uhh, paper, paper, I have a newspaper in my hand, whew that was close!" So Erik pulled his pants down and squatted over the hole after his underpants dropped, he grunted and then let it loose in a torrent of semi solid diariah occaisionally making loud flatuant noises till he was finished and he used the news paper to wipe with tossing it down the hole, then after pulling up his drawers found a wet nap in his pocket and cleaned his hands and tossed it in the hole and wiped his hands on his pants. Then he walked out and downstairs as he was whistling the same tune from before, suddenly stopping in his tracks at the bottom of the stairs as the stench hit his nose and he saw poop smeared all over the bar and the walls and the bar tender and stopped whistling, the Parrot squawked and said "Where were you when the shit hit the fan?" Erik's mouth opened in horror, "uh, forget the tab, uh thanks for uh…." Erik ran out the door, and ran all the way home. Then when he got in he went into the coat closet and sat on the floor with his hands over his head, just then the phone rang. "Oh shit, no, they know where I live" whispered Erik. Momentarily he heard Judith's voice, "Erik it's the Cable company, come to the phone!" "I'm in here, bring me the phone, I'll take it in here" shouted Eric. Judith opened the closet door and handed him the phone, "Yeah, Macintosh here" said Erik. "We really need you to start tomorrow to start training, can you show up at eight in the morning?" said the voice at the other end of the line, "Sure, yeah, super." "Mr. Macintosh, you have the job, congratulations." "Thanks, I'll be there" the other end hung up, Erik then hung up, and started laughing. The closet door swung open "Wooooweeeeee I got the job!" Judith stood there hands on her hips, "Whataya know, my husband finally came out of the closet." "What are you waiting for woman, let's have sex and watch that old Frankenstein sings VHS video tape, tonight the sweet heavenly voice of Candace Tameron while you get to ride the wild stallion!!"Meanwhile back at the Ferral residence Bob the Astral beamer and Green teen were watching BullHouse on television sitting on the couch together in the living room, Bob kept scooting closer to Green and then said, "This is me favorite episode, Danny's hair turns green, and everybody loves everybody." He put his arm around Green, "Oh Bob, your're so romantic, Kiss me you fool!" They french kissed holding each other longingly. "Mmmmmmmm, Chocolatey", said Bob as he pulled away, "Well you know Bob, I am a popular candy" she said. "So is your Candy skin this green shell, or is this what you wear to cover your nakedness?" "Actually Bob I am naked, you just can't tell unless you hold me up to the light like a water mark, here take this flashlight and shine it over my boobs" she said, Bob shone the light on her skin, suddenly her breasts and vagina were visible, "Don't tell anyone Bob, it's a trade secret like the formula for Moca Cola!" Suddenly a knock came from the front door, Bob got up and answered the door. A very angry Oreon cookie stood there fuming at him with his fists clinched, "Irene, I know you're in there you hussy, come out here, you're coming home with me!!" "Ello ello, Green who is this and what the bloody hell is going on around here!?" Said Bob the Astral beamer. "Billy Joe Cornbread you go straight to hell, I'm not coming home with you now or any other time, I'm a star now and I have a boyfriend!!" Shouted Green. "Is that what she's been telling you, that she's your girlfriend and she thinks she's a star!? Pshaw, Ha Ha, C'mon Green Irene the dream is over, tell this creep you're with me and get in the damn car!!" Green turned a little red in the face and jumped off the couch, Listen to me Mr. Oreon cookie, just because I screwed you out of pity does not make me your wife or your girlfriend, is that loser boozer friend of yours EAR MUFF driving the getaway car!? How pathetic, with a name like Muff he has to be a faggot, why don't you two Queers go buttfuck each other and get married and pissoff, because you're crazy if you think I'm going to marry you!"

"Who the hell do you think you're talking to IRENE, I knew you when you were nobody, and that's who you'll always be till you have our baby you abortion loving naked whore!" Shouted Oreon, Green looked as if someone slammed the door in her face and she blanched and bit her lower lip, "listen here you Gomer Pyle wanna be, you damn goober loving butt monkey I was on the pill!" She Sobbed, "Bob, do something" she said in a horse voice as tears streamed down her face, Bob's expression changed from shock to outrage as he stared down at the five foot tall Oreon cookie man, suddenly a black wrist watch appeared out of nowhere on Bob's left wrist, with that hand he pointed his fist at Oreo/Billy Joe and with his other hand touched a stud on the black watch and a laser beam shot out of the watch scorching Billy Joe's big toe on his left foot. "YEEEEEOWW" Screamed Mr. Oreon, Bob only said two words, "run punk.", the Cookie shaped man rolled away to the getaway car as fast as he could shouting "Earmuff, get me outa here!"

Bob slammed the front door and turned to his lady love, "Green darling, it's alright he's gone" said Bob. Green sobbed, "Oh Bob, will it really ever be over?" Bob took her hand in his and said, "it's time to get Mike, there's something fishy going on with the Cosmic balance, and we're going to need all the help we can get love, there's one sure way to get to the bottom of this, and that's team work!" Bob marched over to Mike and Mina's bedroom, and knocked hard on their bedroom door, "Mike, honeymoon's over, we've got work to do!"

Chapter Two

Mike and Mina had just finished lovemaking when they heard Bob's knock at the bedroom door, Mina's eyes began to glow a gold white, and she levitated three feet above the bed, and then settled back down. Mike said in a whisper "Honey, I don't know what's going on but we should get dressed and tell Bob about this." The couple got dressed, and came out of the bedroom, Mike told Bob what happened, and Bob told Mike about the Cosmic balance being off. "So Do you think it has anything to do with Mina?" "Hard to say, she is from another universe, and sex does mix two different quantum flux materials, but if someone like the demon Puck is involved your sister and brother in law are in danger." Green spoke up, "what are we waiting on then, let's charge on over there and rescue them!!"

They all went running out the door. Meanwhile back at Judith's and Erik's the two are in the bedroom naked on the bed watching Candace Tameron slap her boyfriend after he whispers something indecent in her ear, all the while Judith is on top of Erik who is straining his neck to see the TV at the

end of the bed against the wall on the dresser and laughing hysterically, just then they hear the front door slam open and a pounding ensues on the bedroom door. "Erik, Judy, are you in there!?" Comes the voice of Mike, suddenly the door swings open, and Judy screams. "Whoa", says Mike, "I'm blind, I did not want to see that!" Bob the astral beamer whistles a wolf call at her and Judy's face turns red as she grabs the sheet and pulls it around her. Green speaks up, "I bet ya didn't see that cumin,… Pardon the pun." Bob intervenes, "okay, okay, back it up, nothing to see here" Bob makes cat sounds-"R'owww, RR'OW!" Mike closes the door, "Hurry and get decent you guys, we have to discuss something." After about five minutes they came out of the room, "So you see", said Bob "the Cosmic balance has been disturbed, has anything unusual happened?" Judith remarks, "You mean, besides the Smiley face and Green?" Erik's eyes got real wide, "The Vacuum cleaner!" "Wait" Judith exclaimed, "It's in the Coat closet!" Everybody slowly approaches the closet. Erik opened the closet door slowly, the door creaked a high pitch, the door was open and he flicked on the closet light. The Sweeper sat there, Erik touched the on button, suddenly it hummed and beeped, Erik picked up the attachment and pointed it at the wall behind the coats, and a blue ray shined upon the wall. Erik turned off the Sweeper. The Wall glowed blue, until it was replaced by an image of pine trees and snow, they felt the wind gusting against their faces. "Quickly everyone" Said Bob, "put on a Coat and follow me through the portal."

They did as he said, and followed Bob into the dense Pine Forrest, " Where are we Bob?" Asked Judith. "SHSH, The land of Yarnia" Whispered Bob.

"Never heard of it" whispered Mina, "You've never heard of the Lion, Bitch, and Wardrobe?" Asked Bob. "Nope", said Mina, "Fair enough" said Bob. "Mike go back and get the Sweeper" Bob said in a low voice. He did as he was told, "If I'm right we might need that thing's computer" Whispered Bob. They trudged through the snow till they came to a clearing, "What's that?" Asked Green outloud. "SHSHSH,….Obviously it's a lamp post my dear." "Everybody get back, and hide behind the trees" said Bob. They all hid behind the trees, just then a Four foot tall Satyr like imp ran into the clearing with a few small boxes in his arms, stopping to set them down he squatted near the lamp post and defficated on the ground, stood up, picked up his packages and then ran off down a trail. "Well that was disgusting" said Green, "it was more than disgusting, it was the demon Puck! That imp knows something." Said Bob. "Hey guys, what's that noise?" said Green.

Mina spoke up "Hey that sounds like a sleigh, c'mon guys someone's coming, let's run!!" They ran likity split over the snowy pine tree covered hills, "Hurry" said Mike, "they're gaining!" They could hear the sleigh bells getting closer and louder. Suddenly they all fell over a small cliff and flew ass over tea kettle into the snowbank. The sleigh could be heard moving closer as the reindeer approached with their stomping hooves crushing the frozen snow, until abruptly it halted a few feet away.

"What's it look like to you Pop?" said the blonde elf to the brown haired elf,

"It's the darndest thing I ever did see Snap, what do you think crackle?" said the brown haired elf to the black haired elf, just then everybody pulled their heads out of the snow to gaze on the elves in the huge luxury sleigh with it's eight reindeer. Green was the first to speak up, "this snow can't be good for my candy coating". Bob blinked and said "Santa's elves?" Erik and Judith looked at each other and said "why not, we have a talking smiley face and a huge talking green disc candy southern belle." Mina spoke up casting a scowl at Mike, "honey I'm freezing my teets off!" "Here now, what's that? Santa? You're confusing us with the Keeblers, they're one quarter gnome you know, that's why they're so short and runty." Said Snap the blonde elf, Pop the brown haired elf spoke up. "Say Snap, aren't these folks getting a wee bit frost bit in that there snow bank?" the black haired elf Crackle's face lit up and he replied, "Hey guys, why don't we load'em all up in grandma's sleigh and take'em back to our place for a hot cup of Swiss Mrs Cocoa and some of your Krispies with reindeer milk in front of a toasty roaring fire my brothers?" Everyone sitting in the snow shivered trying to shake their heads yes and chorused "y,y,y,yeah!"

Chapter Three

After the gang arrived at the stone cottage in the woods and the Elves put the sleigh in the barn they went inside to thaw & dry out in front of the blazing fire place while the wives of the elves gave them dry clothes. "You drink some of my hot cocoa, ya?" said Snap's wife Helga. "Helga, perhaps our friends would like some of your husband's fried rice with milk and sugar", said Ingrid. "Ya, Ya, Ingrid, strangers get nice and warm and then eat", said Helga. Just then Pop's wife Dorothy brought some blankets to cover them up in their chairs. Mike spoke up after pulling the blanket tightly around himself, "Even the forrest creatures must be freezing, I didn't see as much as a beaver!" Dorothy smiled at that, "oh, you wanna see my brown beaver?"

Pop raised an eyebrow in a Most Vulkan way, "Hey now, you stop that Dorothy, keep your clothes on, that's not funny!" Green coughed and cleared her throat in embarrassment, "I've heard of friendly samaritans, but that is a little over the top man." Snap gestured to his wife, "This is my wife Helga, and my name is Snap." Crackle pointed at his wife and said, "This is my wife Ingrid, and they call me Crackle." Pop gently slapped Dorothy's rear end and said "This is my wife Dorothy, and I'm the only one to take liberties with this vixen, by the way, they call me Pop." Mina could not contain her curiousity " If you're Elves why aren't you short?" Helga snorted a laugh, "That old myth, they're all six and a half feet tall, you're talking about Dwarves and Gnomes!" Dorothy interjected, "Why we're only five feet tall, can you imagine us married to Dwarves?" Ingrid gasped, "oh the scandle." Bob interupted them, "Scyuze me ladies are you sayin that you are Elves too, and if so what would that be in metric?" Snap smiled, "oh no, our wives are human, Helga is Swiss, Ingrid is Swedish, and Dorothy is English, and as for Metric, well, we don't get out much. We're originally from Maine but

our ancestry is Scotch-Irish Pictone, does that answer your question?"
"Quite" said Bob. Pop gestured toward the kitchen table, "please Snap
let our guests sup on some of your Krispy fried rice with reindeer milk
and sugar, it's quite a treat!" Erik stood up and said, "you mean rice

krispies?" Pop frowned, "Yes, that's what I said, just like grandma used
to make in the old country!" They all gathered around the table which
was a long rectangular table with a red and white checkered table cloth,
and they sat down to eat their rice krispies. "You must be strangers
to this neck of the woods my friends, do you not know about the great
Bitch and the devil in the blue dress?" Quizzed Snap looking straight
at Green. "Pal, I'm a huge ass green chocolate that does commercials
and talk shows, I'm from Hollywood, you couldn't get stranger than that
unless you went to the Twilight zone, no offense Bob." Replied Green.
"None taken Darling", said Bob the Astral Beamer. "By the way Snap, I've
brought toilet Paper if anyone's interested", said Bob. Helga clapped her
hands, "Oh joy of joys, now we can test the indoor plumbing darling!"
Mina swallowed a mouthful of rice krispies, "MMMMy, um, tell us more
about this Bitch and her blue devil!" Judith spoke up after finishing her
bowl of rice krispies, "Yes, do tell us more, and what about the demon
Puck?" She finished her question with a loud fart. "oh, hoo hoo hoo, toot
sweet", said Crackle. Judith turned red in the face, "oh excuse me".
Everyone snickered. "Well, we all know about the Bitch and that imp of
a Satyr called Puck, Puck is an agent of Chaos empowered by the Bitch
with the Ouija board and her mystical crystal pendent necklace, as for
the devil in the blue dress, she is the Muse of the Bitch called Queen
Rebecca!" said Snap breathlessly. "You see" said Pop, "Queen Rebecca the
Bitch of Yarnia does doughnuts in people's yards with her jeep that she
drives around in, and her girl friend Donna Joe the Muse tells her knock
knock jokes!" "Oh, but there's hope my friends, let's tell them about
the prophecy, let's tell them about Eliono and his heroes!" exclaimed
Crackle. Dorothy chimed in, "Yes, that old legend tells us that when
Liono and his friends come, Father Christmas will grant a wish for every

loving heart, the heart is the key." Erik spoke up, "uh, where does the vacuum cleaner come into this, there's no place like home." Pop looked at the Vacuum cleaner, "Talk machine, how do we get our friends back home?" The Sweeper hummed electrically, and then spoke in an automated voice, "I am not programmed to respond in that area." "Oh, I know, I know, follow the yellow brick road, the castle is on the other side of the ridge, the snow bank on the other side of Lamp Post clearing is where it begins, just follow the yellow brick road!!" said Dorothy. "Yes, Snap they might find the Wizard of lost causes, the Great Poet Paul!" Bob interjected, "Tally ho lads, and ladies, we're off to see the Wizard!" "There's just one thing, The Bitch lives with him and keeps him prisoner, you'll have to sneak up on them, and I'm afraid we'll have to keep this Vacuum in our broom closet so it won't warn the Queen!"said Snap. "What are we waiting on, let's go!" Erik got up from the table, tossed his blanket aside and turned around and bent over. Then he grabbed his butt cheeks and moved his butt cheeks as if they were speaking, as he shouted out, "TALLY HO!!"

Chapter Four

Our young group of intrepid adventurers set out for the Castle of the Bitch following the yellow brick road, which strangely enough had been shoveled recently of all the snow that covered the path, soon they came upon a frozen field of snow where the path split into two different directions, and an old scare crow was propped up against the wooden fence with a shovel and he appeared to be sleeping. Mina walked up to him and said, "Hey you, who are you and what are you doing out in this cold weather?" "Huh,oh,ACHOOO!" "Sorry about that", "You can just call me Uncle Jesse, everybody does little mamma!" said the scare crow. "I'm dressed this way because it was Halloween and I bought this Scare crow costume my boys picked out, and if I take it off I might freeze. The last thing I remember is that midget that looks like Pan playing a pan pipe when us guys were trick or treating, and then there was this flash of light, the next thing I know I'm tripping over this snow shovel!" "you would've had to been shoveling for two days to uncover this path, what were you thinking?" asked Mike. "I don't know man, it's like I've been in a daze having this weird dream, where are you guys headed, can I come along, I'm freezing my tushy off." Said Uncle Jesse. "Yeah" said Green, "Let's give the kid a break, maybe the Wizard can help him." "Do you think so, cause I need somebody to help straighten out my brain." Replied Uncle Jesse. Erik said, "Well, if the Wizard can help restore the cosmic balance, maybe he can help you with your brain, c'mon, let's go."

The group of friends wandered along the shoveled path for about a mile till they wandered into a grove of pine trees and a shivering tin woodsman with a golf club. "Danny? Danny Danner, is that you? Oh my god man, I thought I'd never see you again!" exclaimed uncle Jesse. "uhhhhh, brrrrr, c, c, c, cold! What took you so-(cough cough cough) long?" replied the tin woodsman golfer. "I knew I should have gone on that blind date, I should never have turned my back on love, I should have had a heart!" retorted Danny. "It's okay man, we're going to see a Wizard, maybe he can give you

a new heart, and give us some fur coats and cough syrup while he's at it." Replied Jesse. "seriously guys we have to g, g, get out of this cold weather, these snot sickels are starting to make my face go numb." Shot back Danny.

"Well", said Bob, We're almost over this ridge it can't be more than two more miles, let's press ahead and follow this yellow brick road!" Danny stared at Bob and Green, "Did that smiley face just speak, and is that a giant chocolate standing next to him?" "I thought they were just hallucinations, but yeah I think you're right, but I'm listening to that smiley face, let's keep moving!" replied Jesse. So the adventurers kept marching along the path like the brave heroes they were, till they came to the bottom of the ridge, where they spotted a man in a lion suit. He stood there holding a plastic light saber up to his face with both hands, he shouted feircely into the wind. "Sword of omens, give me sight beyond sight!" Uncle Jesse yelled at him, "Hey, knuckle head! Who are you supposed to be the cowardly lion or Eliono?"

Danny jumped up excitedly waving his golf club, "It's Joey!!"

Then everybody stood around introducing themselves. Joey said, "Elves? What happened, why didn't they come along?" Bob replied, "Be sensible old chap, they're married, their wives wouldn't stand for it." "Yeah, tell me about it, I used to be married to the ol ball and chain too", said Jesse."I wanna hear more about this Wizard you mentioned," replied Joey, "Maybe he could help my career as a stand up comic". "You never know", said Danny Danner the Tin woodsman. Erik spoke up, "this yellow brick road goes up this embankment past those gnarled giant oaks up ahead, the sooner we get up this hill the sooner we get into the Castle at the top!"

So the brave adventurers headed up the path, only to have a snowball hit Green in the face knocking her on her butt. "Who threw that!?" demanded Danny, just then a snow ball hit him in the chest knocking him down into the snow beside the path, it made a loud thump against his metal costume as he fell backwards. "Green!" shouted Bob the Astral beamer, Jesse said, "Hey, what gives!?" they looked off to the side where about twelve tall trees stood, suddenly they saw that the trees had faces, and one tree was bending down and making a snow ball with branch like hands and arms as it reached down.

"All right punks, this is war" said Joey, "This here Lion aint no coward, I'm gonna go Full Lion on your wooden butts, Thunder brats ho!" shouted Joey as he raised his plastic light saber to the sky. Suddenly the green plastic blade of the Light saber lit up, and there was a flash of green lightning in the sky.

Suddenly out of nowhere, a dark purple light and a scarlet light flashed above the trees, and transformed into super heroes.

The Dark purple light changed into the superhero Static cling, while the scarlet light transformed into the superhero Major Mojo, they came flying through the air with fury, and a single minded determination to drive back the walking trees who were busy making snowballs. Major Mojo Karate kicked one tree on his back side, and landed the tree in the snow with a huge Whump! Static Cling formed an energy paddle and ball in the air, and slapped the energy ball into the lead tree's head knocking him on his face in the snow. The trees bellowed, "retreat, the porcs are too powerful for us!" With that the trees began to scurry away in fear. Static Cling then formed an energy Zap man who started biting the rear end of the tree in the rear who was retreating, while Major Mojo used his super speed to grab up snowballs and pelt the running trees with them as they ran away screaming for help.

Suddenly the wind began turning warm, the snow was beginning to melt, Bob holding Green's hand exclaimed, "Eliono has brought hope into the world and it's affecting the weather, Joey has somehow tapped into this world's magic!" The two heroes introduced themselves to the group, and the group introduced themselves in turn to the super heroes. The friends then marched up the yellow brick path going up the hill, till they came to the very top of the ridge, where finally they beheld the Castle itself.

"Here at last," said Bob, "look, there's the white jeep of the Snow Queen!"

"Let's pay these people a visit, and we will free the Wizard you mentioned," said Feedback. Suddenly they could hear birds tweeting in the background, the snow had all melted by now, the ground was still moist and muddy in some places. "Now that this world has hope her power wanes, and ours grows stronger, come my friends, let us go forward and knock upon her front door." Whispered Major Mojo. The friends went up to the castle, and Feedback knocked on the front door. No one answered, so they opened the door and walked into the main hall, and forward into the throne room.

Chapter Five

Sitting there on the throne sat Queen Rebecca, and on her right sat TJ her niece, Jesse was the first to speak up. "Becky, you mean it's you? Guys, that's my ex wife!" Danny was the next to say something, "TJ! You have a lot of explaining to do young lady! Guys, this is my daughter TJ." Queen Rebecca the snow Queen fixed her gaze upon them and shrilled, "What have

we here my dear, the three Dunces and their band of merry men?! Now I have them where I want them, in my trap!"

Static cling spoke up, standing in brave defiance, his dark uniform making him stand out in the crowd, "Some how miss I don't think it's us that's in trouble, you have some explaining to do!" TJ spoke up, "And who do we have here my lady, my, my, they do have some brass to them!"

"I'm called Static cling" said Static cling as he walked forward to stand in front of the group, then Major Mojo speedily walked to the front to join him, the two heroes bravely guarding the rest, Static cling in his dark uniform, and Major Mojo in his scarlet uniform. Major Mojo stood next to him and crossed his arms, "I'm called Major Mojo, and I think you should answer the man." "Yes, explanations are in order here" replied the Queen, her diamond tiara glistening in the torch light upon her carefully quaffed dark hair, " but first we must deal with the cause of all this hope and goodwill Joey! What about it Cowardly Lion, or should I call you Lion fart? My goodness what an impressive light saber you carry with you, I think we shall have a closer look!" With a motion of her right hand the light saber flew out of Joey's hand and into the Queen's hand, with the other hand she stroked the black crystal pendent hanging from her neck. "Becky what's wrong with you? You would never harm us, we love you, what's happened to you?" pleaded Joey. "Let's just say, since My Ouija board began speaking, I see things in a whole new light, and now I see that the lot of you have come to the end of your road", said the Queen as she grinned wickedly and handed the light saber to DJ, who tossed it behind the throne. "TJ, listen to me, this Halloween nonsense has to stop, I'm your father young lady, and I'm telling you to end this now." said Danny the tin woodsman as he brandished his golf club. "End? Yes, you've met your end," she snickered, Queen Rebecca joined her in laughter and replied, "What a lovely way to end an evening, I have the Wizard in my dungeon, and now you shall join him there as my prisoners, escort them to their doom my love."

Suddenly the group found that their feet were stuck to the floor, Static cling was the first to try and move, "Mojo! I can't move my feet, I'm stuck! Try to move!" Major Mojo tried to move, "My legs, my legs won't move!"

Green Spoke up " I can't move either, Bob can you move?" Bob seemed frozen to one spot hovering above the floor, "I can't budge!" Joey looked at Danny, "Danny we're all stuck, I can't move an inch!" "oh, you'll move alright" said DJ. Suddenly the group of friends all began to behave like marionettes and marched ahead in front of TJ who pranced along in her blue dress gesturing at them with her hands, and off they went into the dungeon where TJ stopped and slammed and locked the door, laughing as she left them to their fate in the dimly lit dungeon illuminated only by a burning torch on the wall. "Where's the Wizard?" asked Mike, Suddenly a loud echoey voice spoke above their heads- "I am here my children, in the corner." They all turned to see a beach ball sized grey sphere sitting on a stone rectangular block which cradled the sphere. "Yes, my children, I am here within this sphere, I am the Wizard of Lost causes, the great poet Paul Fraley, or rather what he shall become three billion years from now at after the end of time." Intoned the megaphone like voice that spoke from above and all around them in the small dungeon.

"How much ya wanna bet this scene is outta Star Heck Mike?" whispered Erik. Mike replied in a low voice, "Fifty Quatlooz". "Wrong episode my son" said the big echoey voice.

Major Mojo walked up to the sphere, "You mean to say, you're imprisoned in this sphere?" asked Major Mojo. "Yes, my son, I am from what you would call the future, when I was in heaven's Akashic Library reading about your history I found myself pulled into it's astral spaces, thus came I to be here in your time." Said the Wizard. "You must know the outcome of this situation then!" exclaimed Major Mojo. "Yes, I'm afraid that after you are locked into this dungeon you resort to canabalism and after only one person is left he dies of starvation." Replied the Wizard. Danny spoke up, " which one is the last one alive?" "Joey" replied the Wizard.

"JOEY!!!!!" Yelled everybody, Joey looked around with a guilty expression,

"I didn't eat dinner." "RRRRRRRR" growled his stomach. Major Mojo's eyes went wide, "No, I can't believe that, there must be something different this time, we can't let that happen!" He said as he gripped the sphere with both hands lifting it up out of it's cradle. Suddenly the sphere slipped out of his grasp and hit the floor bouncing, making spring like bouncing noises as it bounced on the floor. "Owch"- Boing- "Owch" – Boing – "Owch" – Boing – "Owch" – Boing – "Owch"!!! Major Mojo caught the Sphere in his hands and put it back in it's stone cradle, at that moment the sphere flashed green and there was a high pitched whine, and then the green light was coming from Major Mojo till the Whine stopped. Major Mojo/Wizard now spoke with the echoing megaphone like voice- "Yes my children, there is something different, in the history book I read I was not in this story, somehow my presence here has changed history so that this time Evil will not concqor the forces of good, this time you will not die. Because I am with you everything will work out for the best." Said Mojo/Wizard. "Mojo, what are you saying? Are you saying you're the Wizard? What have you done with Major Mojo?!" asked a shocked

Static cling. "Have no fear, he is still here, we share consciousness within this body, he sleeps while I inhabit his body my son." Joey walks up to Mojo/Wizard, "Do you think you can get me back BJ's Light saber Mr. Wizard?" asked Joey as he started to lean against the sphere. "Sure son" said Mojo/Wizard "but call me Paul". Just then Joey leaned against the sphere and it fell off it's stand and hit the floor bouncing till it split into pieces. Boing- Boing- Boing- Crack. Everybody shouted at Joey "JOEY!!" Jesse walked up to Joseph/Lion fart "Ya big goof, now look at what you did!" Joey looked at Jesse, "OOPSSY". "it's alright, if we can break the demonic power possessing Becky and TJ father Christmas will grant our wishes and then I can go home to the future to the new heaven and new earth, what you have to do is get their Ouija board and destroy it, it should be behind her throne on the floor!" replied Mojo/Wizard. Static Cling scratched his head, "yeah, okay, but how do we get out of this room Paul?" Mojo/Wizard walked up to Danny, "The golf club if you don't mind my friend."said Mojo/Wizard, Danny handed him the golf club, and Mojo/Wizard propped it up against the door so the club end was touching the area near the slide bolt on the other side of the door. "Static cling, remember that game space crusaders with the energy bolts from the space

ship? If you can hit the floor at the bottom here where the top of the club rests against the floor, the electrical current will travel up the length of the club hitting the slide bolt on the other side popping out the part that the bolt fits into, and presto- we're free!" said Mojo/Wizard. Bob said, "I like that plan." "You see, if Danny had brought an axe instead of a golf club the Queen would have confiscated it and we'd all be doomed. Funny how things work out."said Mojo/Wizard. Static cling replied, "Okay everybody, step back, here goes!" Everyone stepped back, and Static cling generated an energy image of a space ship that fired a shot at the base of the club on the floor, the current shot up the club and there was a loud sizzle and Pop, the door swung open! " "Erik, I need you to go in the throne room and provide a distraction, Feedback and I will Follow, when I grab the Ouija board and toss it in the open Feedback will blast it, and we'll all be rid of this black magic, and TJ and Rebecca will be back to normal!" whispered Mojo/Wizard in his megaphone like voice. Mike whispered back, "What about us?" "You guys hang back till we're done." Replied Mojo/Wizard. Then they all went out into the hall, Mojo/Wizard and Static cling, and Erik tip toed into the archway that opens up into the throne room. "Psst, Erik, go." Whispered Static cling. Erik lurked into the throne room slowly careful not to make any noise, he could see TJ and Queen Rebecca talking, he got a little closer, then he turned around and bent over and grabbed his butt cheeks, making them move as if his butt was talking and said really loud- "Mighty Louse is here to save the day", finishing it off with a jungle call,………………. "AHHHHEEAHHHHEEAH!" Since he was off to the side of the room they didn't see Static cling and Mojo/Wizard at first sneaking into the room at the other side of the room slinking along the wall, by the time they spotted Static cling, Mojo/Wizard used his super speed to get behind the throne, grabbed the Ouija board and it's planchette and tossed them out where Feedback could see them. Immediately Feedback formed a Ms. Zapman and it gobbled up the Ouija board and the planchette. Suddenly there was a clap of thunder and a wind blew out of nowhere as a demonic scream from above filled the castle's throne room. Then all was silent. Everybody hiding in the archway came out of their hiding spot and walked into the throne room. Erik stood up, turned around, and walked up to Judith. TJ looked around blinking her eyes, "what's going on around here, Dad is that you? How did we get here?" Queen Rebecca sneered, "Well, it looks like my ex husband's band of misfits have won the day, but you haven't won yet!" She looked at TJ and said "I'll get you my pretty!" Just then Mojo/Wizard rushed out from behind the throne with super speed and grabbed the Black crystal pendent off her neck, snapping the necklace and threw it toward Static cling's Ms. Zapman. "Destroy it!" Shouted Mojo/Wizard. Static cling concentrated and then Ms. zapman gobbled up the black crystal and then Rebecca fainted.

TJ tried to revive her aunt Becky, "Dad, why was aunt Becky being so mean? What's going on here?" Rebecca slowly came to as Jesse helped her to stand, "Jesse? What are you doing here?" "coming to your rescue my Queen, can you ever forgive me, will you take me back my darling?"said Jesse in a soft kind voice. "Jesse, you want me- to marry me all over again?"asked Rebecca, "Yes baby" he said with tears in his eyes, "that's what I'm saying" " Wait a minute guys, how do we get home?" asked Danny. "Hmmmmm," said Mojo/ Wizard, "why don't we go out back and ask the great Rubbish heap??" "Oh, I get it, Fragile Rock!" exclaimed Joey.

So everyone went outside and around the back to the courtyard in the rear where they discovered the great Rubbish heap. The Sun was just coming up over the horizon. "Your Rubbish Heapness, er Majesty, Hello!" said Joey.

The Rubbish heap opened her eyes, "MMMMMAhem," She made smacking noises with her mouth, and yawned. "What, What do you want?" she asked.

"We all wish to go home and bring this story to an end your Majesty", said Mojo/Wizard in his voice that still echoed from Mojo's mouth.

"For a piece of garbage I will give you what you seek." Said the Rubbish heap in an elderly lady's voice. Joey looked in his pocket and pulled out a gum wrapper with a piece of gum in it, "Will this used piece of gum do?" asked Joey, "Eh, sure, why not?" said the Rubbish heap. He tossed it into the Rubbish heap. "Paul and TJ must make the journey together to the southern end of the ridge, there lies the table of stone created for the deep magic, the heart is the key, for hope will set you free."said the Rubbish heap, "And take a blanket for goodness sakes, it's a bit nippy, the trash heap has spoken." TJ and Mojo/Wizard looked at each other and shrugged their shoulders, and then walked south toward the end of the ridge with the blanket her father gave her. Finally they found the table, and sat on it's edge.

Back at the Castle however, the demon Puck was sneaking around, and Static Cling spotted him peeing in the rose bushes. So he pointed it out to Bob,

Bob whipped out his magic trumpet and blew a tune toward the sky. Suddenly there were a hundred Smiley faces in the sky buzzing down toward the Dwarf Puck. Bob fiddled with a control knob on his belt and the group of flying Smiley faces began playing the Bloody red baron song, and they threw scads of toilet paper rolls at the Imp Puck, eventually he was tripping over the toilet paper as he ran for cover until one roll of toilet paper hit him in the face and he vanished in a puff of white smoke, the band of smiley faces soared through the air arcing upward and vanished in a flash of gold light. Meanwhile back at the stone table TJ and Paul were lying on the table under the blanket and Paul was kissing her face, and then they went under the blanket as he was tickling her. Suddenly the table cracked! "Crack!" "What happened?" asked Mojo/Wizard, "It is written on the stone table that should anyone fool around on the stone table it will crack, and they will realize their dreams." Said TJ. Suddenly a Spaceship bearing the name U.S.S. Quarx floated down out of the sky and landed not too far from the stone table, "Thank you Paul, you've saved us." Said TJ as she hugged Mojo/Wizard and then he glowed a bright green, and then returned to normal. "What, what's going on?" asked Major Mojo, "I was touching the sphere, then I felt the Wizard touch me on the shoulder and I fell asleep, and now I'm here with you, what has happened?" "A special friend has found a way to send us home, and in so doing was sent home himself", said TJ. "Let's go tell the gang!" she exclaimed. So they went back to the castle and told them, they even found some old tarp to drag the Rubbish heap along into the cargo bay of the space ship, and with that they took off for the home of the Danners and their friends, finally dropping off Danny, TJ, Rebecca, Jesse, and Joey with his light saber, and the two super heroes flew up into the sky and teleported back to their homes, and the space ship then flew up into the heavens. Bob sat at the controls talking to his friends,

"I finally understand it now mates, this Yarnia, it's all a part of the never ending story," with that he reached into his sleeve and pulled out a tape cassette and popped it into a tape player in the computer console and hit play, it began playing Juke box hero. And Mike, Mina, Judith, Erik, Green and Bob flew into outer Space in their spaceship becoming a part of the never ending story- but that's a whole new story in itself.

Thee End.

__"The Powers that be; all's well that ends well. By Paul Fraley ©

ACT - 3. ALLS WELL THAT ENDS WELL.

Chapter One

The Great Space ship Quarx sailed on through the dark nebula. Meanwhile the great Shith Space craft was yanked out of it's tight orbit by the cosmic imbalance between good and evil, since history had been changed, the black hole at the center of the Milky Way galaxy lost some of it's strength temporarily, just long enough to free the Intergalactic Starship that was a frozen grave yard of reptilian fiends from the world of Cylon. The ship was nudged into a higher elliptical orbit thus pushing it farther away from the center of the galaxy, bringing it close to the Fabrini star system. On the world of Cromnus II, the twin Eurodor moons one blue, the other green rose above the night time horizon, and the Crown of Kandorien sat on a troubled Dwarven brow, the great Kandu people mourned the loss of their High Priestess the Queen Mother, who had been devoured by the Halevi Flower that prowls the jungle by night. It was the Last of it's kind, but so was the Queen mother, King Temlok hated the idea of hunting it down to kill it, it was a rare creature of legend said to be wise beyond comparison, the unfertilized juju berries it layed were a staple food for his people since it's mate was dead so the berries could never be fertilized to grow new Halevi flowers. It had become part of their culture, this was a bad omen indeed!

If only the Maize forests could be harvested, but the maize was too small and hard to eat, it was said that the Chumba Wumba the gods of the Kandu planted these forests after coming down from heaven, and then flew away to the yellow star called Helios. The Chicken bones warned him that the appearance of the strange tall girl would herald the great battle between good and evil, the name Winnie Burp was alien so therefore she must be from the world of spirits, her words were strange too. Wolfram and heart, Agent and Illyria, these words she sputtered over and over again when they found her in the Maize forest, now she busied herself with herbs and potions like some kind of witch, yes she was deffinately from the spirit world alright thought Temlok. Imilaya his first wife complained about the smell coming from Winnie's hut, but Temlok did not wish to offend the gods, he half suspected that she did it just to come between him and his second wife

Feylula whose breasts he had been stroking when Imilaya burst in on them complaining about the smells from the neighboring grass hut. Eurodor looked down upon Winnie with kindness, for if Winnie was essential to the defeating the powers of evil, Temlok felt he'd be damned if anything were to happen to her while he was king, she could milk all the chickens in his kingdom for all he cared, That milk though tasted God awful and kept him awake for days after taking just a sip, but it did manage to heal the bruise on his wrist from the rope where the pillar in the temple ruins had to be pulled upright. His people were competent engineers but the temple was holy and only the king should move those sacred stones and marble pillars, the symbol of The chumba Wumba sky king stood proudly on it's huge pedestal holding the star of Helios on his back, the golden statue towered fifty feet into the sky in front of the ancient temple. Temlok feared he would never see the day when his priests would ever use it again.

Meanwhile the great Crocodon the Flag ship of the ancient Cylon empire warped it's way through space and came out of warp in the upper atmosphere of Cromnus II and crash landed on the Scooby coast, the continent of Scooby was vast and the Telorian mountain range divided the coast to the south from the Maize forest in the Kandu kingdom, The ancient Shith Lord of Cylon cast his hungry gaze toward the north with the evil intention of conquest. He was the only Flesh and blood Cylon left alive, the Cylons acompanying him were all robots, they were a bipedal race, The Shit lord was a descendent of the Gorn velociraptors a species of reptile that walked upright. Their racial imperitive was simple erase all existence of the Mammelian races and rule the cosmos. There was an ancient Chumba Wumba legend his robot officers informed him of this world, a path through these mountains built by the Chumba Wumba priests, the Mahktar.

"We'll see whose race is the greatest, those Mahktar have their uses after all, but now the Master race shall devour this world, and that Master would be me, Lord of the house of Shit."thought the Shith Lord outloud, the Robot general responded by saying, "By your command."

Back on the Space ship Quack…….Green sat at the console typing in coordinates to the auto pilot, "Run that by me again Bob?" said Green.

"The coordinates to the source world of the Mahktar, the legendary starcharts will be found in a memory cartridge, it will help me map out the rest of the multiverse, said Bob the Astral beamer." Erik cut in, "Yeah, that's fine for you, don't forget your promise to get us back home." "You're right mate, a promise is a promise, as soon as we get those star charts, we're off to send you back home, why, are you guys getting tired of this adventure?" Queried Bob. "Oh that's fine bob, just don't forget we have lives to go back to." Said Mike. "Alright then, you don't have to get snippity about it." Replied Bob. Boop, Boop, Boop, went the computer scanner. "That's odd", said Bob, "on board sensors detect an additional life form aboard the ship".

"It's kind of odd that it happens on the same day that Mina woke up with a sick tummy, could there be a connection?" asked Mike. Green reached into her duffle bag and pulled out a multipurpose scanner, "let's scan her and find out" replied Green the Candy Queen. "MEEEEEEP!!" went the scanner,

"Oh dear!!" said Green, "what is it!?" Shouted Mike as Green passed the Scanner over Mina, "She's Pregnant!" Bob had his feet on the console, which usually you never saw, then he jumped down from his seat accidently htting a button on the console as his legs became invisible again, the tape machine began playing Huwey Lewis's song Perfect world. "That's incredible!" shouted Bob, "Pregnant, yeah that's incredible" replied Mike, "It's wonderful" exclaimed Judith, "No, I mean The sensors have detected the Mahktar Source world, hang on kids we're going through an asteroid belt!" The ship dipped up and down, zigged and zagged, then arced inward toward the planet as it left the Asteroid field behind, and then plummeted into the atmosphere. Bob shouted over the music, "Breaking rockets on!"

Eventually the song by Huwey Lewis stopped and the ship skidded to a halt in a giant corn field that stretched out on both sides for miles. "Whoa", said Bob, "Ozone build up in the cargo tank", said Bob. "What does that mean?" asked Judith, "It means uhm, gr, tsh, fah" mumbled Bob. "What was that?" asked Mina, "It means the great rubbish heap farts Ozone!" replied Bob. Everyone cracked up laughing, "I'm hitting the pressure release valve and circulating the air in there." He said red faced. After laughing for about six or seven minutes the crew disembarked to explore their world, the sun was just coming up warming the air causing a small mist around the ship. "Bob, listen what's that?" said Mike, "Bok,……Bok, Bok, ……Bok, Bok, Bok", went the odd sound near the ship. Suddenly out of the shadows a huge Chicken came strutting into the light. Mike started laughing, "Erik, look! HA HA HA!" Erik looked dumbfounded, "They've got Tits! Hee Hee Hee!"

They both laughed hysterically, Green shot Bob a look. "What!?" said Bob, "so they've got boobs", Green scowled and said, "Men!" Judith and Mina's jaws dropped open, blinking Mina suddenly said, "Oh m'God, I've got morning sickness again, guys, I'm getting back inside!" "Erik, put your eyeballs back in your head, they're chickens!!" yelled a frustrated Judith, she turned and followed Mina back into the ship. Green said, "Bob keep in touch with your wrist radio, I'm going back inside to check the fuel gauge and primary launch circuits", "right you are love" said Bob softly. Green then went back inside the ship with the other women. "Well, if you two jokers are done laughing, we need to look for a clearing for signs of civilization to find that computer chip hidden by the Mahktar, c'mon let's go."said Bob. "Say", said Mike, what's with all this corn, "Sort of reminds me of Indiana in the spring, wrong time of year for corn." "keep in mind that this is an alien planet" said Bob, "The radiation keeps the corn from maturing but causes extensive stalk growth, basically it's a corn forrest." "Hey, anybody bring any butter? Popcorn city man." Said Erik, "Radiation Erik, you'd break a tooth." Replied Bob. They began walking away from the ship. As they walked for about half a mile, they saw a clearing and a huge stone well, and in the distance they could see grass huts with people moving about, "Well," said Bob, "Civilization at last". Suddenly they were surrounded on all sides by midgets in Squirrel skins brandishing knives and clubs, and bow and arrows. Then it opened up as King Temlok made his way through the crowd, "I am Temlok, king of Dwarves, and I can think of many reasons right now why I would not want to be you, tall ones! First because I am king." He clapped his hands together, and then they started introducing themselves. "Arkloo", "Pogo", "Thromp", "Shivo", "Igloru", "Yowee",

"Therin", "Saabo", "Taabo", "Shamyam"! "Secondly" Went on Temlok, because there are more of us than you". He clapped his hands again, and they resumed introducing themselves. "Shekilo", "Zygone", "Cheribok",

"Buklandar", "Arshugruh", "Ketrelru", "Chubos", "Mekelo", "Arfash",

"Mazax"! "Thirdly" went on Temlok "Our people have a claim on this land, because it was a gift of the Chumba Wumba". Again he clapped his hands, they resumed introducing themselves. "Gunja", "Munba", "Tiewacko", "Charoop", "Lendak", "Eshlasht", "Riujkep", "Smeiyepi", "Yebili", "Swee"! "Fourthly" went on Temlok, "We don't much trust strangers".

He clapped his hands again, they resumed introducing themselves. "Rojo",

"fesujey", "Klozag", "Faijax", "Soruj", "Tobo", "Tebu", "Zedu", "Runja", "Armu"! "Fifthly, and most importantly, these warriors are the best of the best, they are trained for obeidience and for killing, and they're very good at what they do!" rambled Temlok, and for the fifth time he clapped his hands, and the remainder of the small armed crowd finished introducing themselves. "Sheekaru", "Temolar", "Zaznahk", "Orbiru", "Jusho", "Tyrok", "Nytok", "Shuugahn", "Yodu", "Vengi"! They all then let out a growl with grimacing teeth bared at Bob and Erik, "So", said Temlok, "unless you can explain what you're doing here in such a way as not to make me very angry, you might be in for a world of hurt!" Bob, Mike and Erik swallowed really hard, "Gulp", "Gulp", "Gulp".

Just then a robot approached from the mountains on the far side of the village and it was shooting up the place with a laser blaster in it's hand.

Suddenly Bob was wearing a ten gallon Cowboy hat, he spoke into his wrist communicator to Green. "Green my love, put in Flaming Star by Elvis Presley written by Sherman Edwards and Syd Layne, it's marked oldies, and pipe it through darling, the situation looks grim." Suddenly out of nowhere the song Flaming Star began playing, the warriors scattered as the robot shot at them, "Keep down Erik" shouted Bob, as he aimed his wrist laser at the robot and fired. "ZZZZAP!" went the beam as it hit the robot knocking him back. The robot retreated at a furious pace. Mike crouched behind Bob.

Chapter Two

Temlok's warriors rallied around Mike, Erik and Bob, and cheered, Erik had peed in his pants out of fear and everyone pointed and laughed. "I have an overactive bladder!" shouted Erik, Temlok spoke, "You have fought bravely nonetheless and saved our village, you are hereby now accepted as members of the tribe. The strangers are free to go, but tell me strangers who are you and what are you doing here in our land?" Erik cleared his throat, "We are travelers, My name is Erik, this is Bob and Mike, and aboard our space craft er, our heavenly chariot, are the women Mina, Judith, and Green, and the great trash heap who is wise beyond measure." "way to go Erik, now they're going to think we're lunatics" said Mike. Bob turned to Mike, "See that old abandoned temple ruin in the distance next to the village? I have an idea." He spoke into his wrist communicator, "Green listen carefully, take off and hover over the clearing where the old ruins are and drop off the great trash heap, just do it, don't ask." "Gotcha Bob", said Green, the next couple of minutes there was a loud whirring and the ship flew overhead and dropped off the great trash heap in the middle of the ancient ruins in a roofless temple. The ship then flew back to it's original cooridinates in the corn forrest. Temlok watched with interest, "What is the meaning of this my friends, why drop trash heap in the temple of our Mahktar gods the priests of our gods the Chumba Wumba?Explain!"

Bob spoke up, "This is our gift to you great chief, this is no ordinary trash heap, she lives, it is a living rubbish heap who answers all questions put to it with great wisdom, all one must do is deposit a piece of trash to feed her and you will have her as your oracle, a symbol of our eternal friendship!"

"It is good, I will toss an old loin cloth onto the rubbish heap, and if what you say is true, we will know who our enemy is!" replied Temlok.

Temlok approached the rubbish heap with an old squirrel skin loin cloth and tossed it on the rubbish heap, " Tell me great rubbish heap, who is this new enemy?" " Thanks sonny, yes, well now then, this new enemy is what is left of the old Cylom empire, it is the great Lizard King of the house of Shith, and his goal is to kill all mammal life forms, that would include you sweety. The great rubbish heap has spoken!" The Granny like face of the rubbish heap burped and then closed her eyes. The chief of the Kandu walked into the center of the village grass huts, where Mike, Erik, and Bob were waiting, sitting on some bamboo couches near the Fire pit. Temlok spoke, "It is obvious what we must do, we must perform the Kandu war chant," Temlok smiled, "Which also happens to be the Kandu love chant"! The tribe cheered, all the Dwarf women hurried into the grass huts, while the Male dwarves pulled out some "Old Spice cologne" out of cubby holes outside the huts and put some on, "A gift of the Mahktar" explained Temlok, "Now let the fun begin!" shouted Temlok, suddenly then the male dwarves all went into the grass huts and in the next few seconds the huts were all shaking up and down and back and forth, "If the hut is rockin, don't come a knockin!" laughed Temlok outloud. Then the singing began, in rythym with the vibration and shaking of the gras huts, "say" said Mike, "I know that tune, it's Mahna-Mahna, the Piero Umiliani song, by Edwards B. Marks music company!" "an oldie but a goody" said Erik, " Wooo, It's got a beat and you can dance to it"! said Bob.

Just then The girl named Winnie came out and sat next to them, "Hi, my name is Winnie, so you're from out of town?" Just then the warriors came out and kissed their sweeties goodbye and went with weapons in hand toward the mountains after their enemy. It was close to noon so the group decided to look for firewood which was sparse but they found some already chopped and waiting near some huts, and prepared the fire pit for when the sun would go down, "It starts to get dark around here after about five thirty, sundown occurs around six thirty –five according to my watch, so in addition to this wood we should also grab a few shucks of this useless corn to make a big fire in the fire pit." Said Winnie to Erik. So after about an hour and a half the gang had a huge pile of wood and corn shucks sitting near the fire pit, and they were all getting cozy talking about all sorts of things, such as time dialation for space ships. It was about two thirty by the time they were all settled in and engrossed in this conversation. Mina signaled Bob, "Yeah, you left the com link on, we overheard what you were saying about time travel, remember that movie Back to future world? The Martin letter never would have happened if Thomas Edison had not traveled back in time, the Martin letter is the key, so time travel back to the past might attract Astral beamers! So maybe you should consult your great Ashtray." "That's rubbish heap" said Bob, "Yeah, right, consult the trash heap, same thing." Right about that time Dwarven warriors began showing up panting and screaming, "Lightning bolts, it throws lightning bolts!" yelled the warriors. So they went up to the great trash heap and tossed a dirty handkerchief that Mike had in his pocket

into the trashheap, and asked "What can you tell us about our enemy?"

"Oh sweeties it all began with the Cylon conspiracy, as you full well know, global conspiracies are very dangerous things to muck about with! The best way to stop a global conspiracy is to A: expose the guilty parties in power. B: Anticipate the guilty party's in power attempt to exterminate the exposers. C: send in Assassins at the time they try to destroy the exposers- timing must be perfect. D: set up spies to relocate exposers, recruit them as spies with new identities. Result, head Cylom of the house of Shith goes into hybernation- if he finds the Eye of Jupiter, the weapon of Merlin- Mankind as you know it will become extinct. What you need darlings is a hero, say perhaps a Super chicken like Erik hopped up on Chicken milk, ask Winnie she will explain it to you!" Erik flexed his muscles "Does Tom Hanks love his dog, does Malcolm McDowel have a thing for poodles, Does Jay Leno look good in an eye patch, of course I want to play the part of the hero, and avoid the chewy chunks of degredation! Point the the way, I'm smokin!" exclaimed Erik. So they all climbed down from the temple steps and walked back to the fire pit, so Winnie told them about her secret sauce made from hot spices and chicken milk for super strength, and then went back to get some from her hut. Then her giant pet poodle came along with it's saddle and riding gear, it was the height of one of earth's horses, by the time Winnie got back it was sniffing her friends and then with it's rear end facing Erik something embarrassing happened. Winnie held up the bottle of potion, "If I give you this super sauce you have to promise to take me back to earth and drop me off in Los Angeles, Okay?" " Sure thing kido" said Erik, "Let me have it, lay that stinker on me, I'm good for it don't ya know!" shouted Erik, just at that moment the giant poodle broke wind- "FFFFFFFpoooooofffffff!"

The giant poodle fart hit Erik right in the face, "Ggghgghhgghhgasp, bluhhk! Can't breath, eyes watering, can't see, oh god, what is that, nerve gas!?"

Everyone laughed, "Winnie replied, "oh, that's just my poodle sparky, he must have a little gas on his tummy". "I'm not smokin, nobody light a match!" said Erik as he ran around in circles, "Fresh air, must have fresh air now!" gasped Erik as he moved away from the poodle. "Okay, We'll take you to your earth, and drop you off in Los Angeles" Shouted Erik, "But the poodle stays behind Man!" "Sounds fair, so it's a deal then" said Winnie, "Give me the secret super sauce Winnie!"snapped Erik. Bob snickered and touched a button on his belt playing the theme song to the cartoon super chicken as Erik drank down the potion in one gulp. Erik started flapping his arms like a chicken and said in a gasping breath, "God that's hot and spicey!" Suddenly Erik jumped like superman up on the poodle in the saddle and rode away to the mountain pass leading to the Cylom space craft. By that time the super chicken song had played out. Mike looked at Bob, "Well, it's better him than me, if he's not back in two or three hours we send a posse out looking for him." Said Mike. "Sounds fair to me", said Bob.

Meanwhile the dark lord of Shith was instructing his robots to break out a clone canister and put the specimen under the mutato ray in the ship's laboratory. Those stupid Dwarves would pay for their treachery vowed the Lizard king as he paced back and forth, "oh great god of darkness Iblis, give me the power I seek, help me to destroy all of mankind!" prayed the dark Lord of Shith. He paced for a good hour or more, and then a poodle appeared on the horizon.

Chapter Three

Then suddenly The Lizard King the lord of Shith started to make out the figure of a rider on the poodle in the distance, "That's it, get a little closer" mumbled the tarsil mouth Lizard King, "Have I got a surprize for you."

The brave rider approached the ship, till he felt he was close enough, and brought the poodle to a halt. "So, you're the Lizard King from planet Cylom?" asked Erik. "Yes, but if you prefer an Earth name, call me Clarence after one of your popular fairy tales after all, it is Christmas. Oh I know what you're going to say, what you fail to realize is that earth's radio broadcasts have been beaming out into space for centuries, that's how I am able to reference movies like it's a wonderful life, or music like Lord have mercy on my soul, by black oak Arkansas." Replied the bipedal lizard as he turned a switch on his belt, and Lord have mercy on my soul began playing on the ship's loud speaker. "We were once the Master race in this galaxy, the slave race Sleeshak disapeared into the xantha time vortex, they were from the world of Unas, but we were discussing you, weren't we? What to do with you………" "What could itty bitty Clarence do to me?" retorted Erik. "Here is your answer Warm blooded one!" He reached forward and a lightning bolt shot out from his hand striking the feet of the Poodle. The poodle reared back and threw Erik to the ground, and ran back home through the mountain pass. "I wouldn't move from that spot if I were you my two loyal Cylom robots have a bead on you, one has a truth ray in his hand, the other a death ray, no you're not going anywhere, you're going to stay right here and do as I command, because now you're my bitch, Yes, I can mingle with your kind with help from my holographic projector, if I choose I can look like a preacher on Sunday if it suits my purpose, but I've always had a sweet tooth, I've often wondered what it would be like to be a Baker and make cakes and pastries. Emperor Clarence Baker, yes you can address me as such if you wish, anything with the title King in it." "Look, Lizard King, I don't care what your name is, your secret identity or whatever, I came here to tell you to take a hike, hit the road, do not pass go, do not collect two hundred dollars!" retorted Erik. "Hit him with the truth ray unit two", said Clarence Baker the Lizard King, "By your command", said the robot. The pink strobing laser shot out and singed Erik's forehead and shut off. SSSSSSS! Went the beam, "Ow, you cruel bastard!" shouted Erik. "You really think I'm a cruel Bastard?" "Yes", replied Erik. The beast laughed, "Well, at least we know that's not a lie, what is your name?" Erik began to sweat and shake, "M, My name is Erik……" "Tell me Erik, why are you so brave?"

"I took something, a potion, to make me invincable" replied Erik, The Lizard King smiled "You did what? Ha Ha Ha!" The Lizard King couldn't stop laughing, finally he stopped and said "When you stop amusing me and can tell me nothing more, you are going to die." "I'm as strong as ten of you right now" growled Erik, "but that isn't the issue is it now boy, I can do whatever I want to you, and you can't stop me! Tell me a lie, Tell me that you're the Lizard King", replied Clarence the Lord of Shith. "I'mmm, ahhhhh, My name is Erik, it's like I'm in some kind of hypnotic trance", said Erik. "Yes, it prevents you from telling a lie, that beam that hit you is technology based on transporter technology, I'm afraid it was carrying some unusual bacteria, if I repeat the process there will eventually be brain damage dear boy." "I can still resist you!" Erik said, "ah, it seems whatever potion you drank failed to enhance your intellect, yes by all means resist, and I shall strike you with my lightning bolts, and should you start running away my other robot with the death ray is a crack shot, you'll die in seconds!" Erik stepped back and turned looking towards the mountains,

"Help!! Somebody help me!" screamed Erik. "Erik turn around and take off your clothes, Do it!" shouted Clarence the Lizard King, "Wha, What? You sick perverted freak, what did you say?!" replied Erik, The Lizard king pointed a finger at Erik's foot and a lightning bolt arced from his finger to that spot,

ZZZAP! Erik fell back on his butt, "Do what I tell you warm blood, take off all of your clothes!" shouted the Lizard King, Erik complied shaking all that time like a leaf. "Stand up and let me see you boy, let's see how big your tally wacker is" Erik stood there shaking and sweating, "That's the little nub you pleasure your females with? Ha, Ha! Diddle with it, pleasure yourself and make it bigger, this is very Entertaining!" Said the Lizard King, "Clarence you ugly turd I've had about enough of you!" shouted Erik, the Lizard King threw another lightning bolt at him missing him by an inch, "If he does that again kill him" said The Lizard King, "Stop back talking me and masturbate or so help me god of darkness you will pay Erik, do it now! Don't just stand there you worm do what I said!" Erik yelled at the top of his lungs, "Rape! Rape! Somebody help me" ! Erik began to sob and a tear ran down his face, "damn chewy chunks of degredation." Whispered Erik as he hid his genitals with his hands, the beast flipped the switch and the song Lord have mercy began to play again, "Don't make me repeat myself punk, Masterbate!"yelled the Lizard King, Erik shaking and his nose starting to drip said "Yes, Master…." Erik complied with the wishes of Clarence Baker the Lord of Shith, and the Lizard King licked his lips with his snake like tongue. "Please, can I stop now and have my underpants?" "What was that punk, did you forget to say Master?"

"Master, can I stop and put my underpants back on?" "Alright my little fairy, put your underpants back on and stop diddling yourself like that, that sort of thing makes hairy palms and you might go blind, Ha, Ha, Ha, Ha!" Laughed the man dragon, "You see Erik, you are a broken man, I know how to break men's spirits because in the end I am a god and you are nothing," said the huge reptile, he took a cartridge from his belt and tossed it down at his feet, and said "Here is the key to my ship, are you man enough to take it from me? No, you're no longer a man, you're a pathetic worm! Isn't that right Erik?!" said the Lizard King. "Yes, Master", said Erik. "See? Isn't it easier now admitting that you're inferior to me?" asked the Lizard King. "Yes Master" Whimpered Erik, now strike some poses like a muscle man, like a body builder and strut around for me but stay close my pretty." Erik complied, and a lot of time was going by, he was beginning to wonder if anyone back at camp was going to miss him, and again the Lizard king played that song Lord have mercy on my soul, Erik was beginning to realize he was doing it to make him lose hope. "Master, may I have my clothes back, it's getting late in the day and I'm getting cold" complained Erik. "Yes, little man put your clothes back on, at least you will die with some dignity, HHHAA Ha Ha Ha Ha, hee hee, hee, ho, ho ho, woooeee!!" exclaimed the Lizard King, Erik began coughing and wheezing as he dressed himself, "Ahh, the Truth ray is beginning to wear off, the microbes have worked themselves into your lungs by now, sorry but each time I blast you with the truth ray, the asthma will get worse and worse as the ray wears off.

I know what we can do for entertainment, do a river dance for me, and when you're done we'll begin again with the truth ray!"hissed the man dragon, sneering at him as he did so. Mean while back at the camp around four thirty in the afternoon the poodle limped it's way back toward the firepit.

Everyone suddenly turned pale when they saw the poodle limp up to Winnie whimpering and lying down at her feet, Mike looked at Bob uncomfortably,

"Do you think he's dead?" asked Mike, "The trash heap has never been wrong before, I don't understand it, he's supposed to become a hero!" whispered Bob. Bob touched his wrist com, "Uh, Green love we've got some bad news for Judith, Erik never made it back…" "What? Okay I don't have to tell her she's right here", "Bob where's my husband?" whimpered Judith, a tear went down Bob's face and he sniffed and said "He might be dead love, I'm sorry." Replied Bob over the com link, "oh God No! No! No! you bring him back to me Bob, bring back my baby please!" Cried Judith hysterically. Bob shut off the com link, "Shut up Bob, let me think!" said Mike, "Can you bring our boy back alive ?" "Yes, Mike I will bring Erik back alive or there will be hell to pay, I'm a pretty good shot with my wrist laser, if for some reason neither one of us returns I want you to know the ship has a phaser bank capable of destroying a city, Don't worry I'll bring the lad back as good as new. Good always wins in the end."said Bob as they both patted each other on the back, Bob walked up to the poodle and lay his hand on the dog's head, "come on old friend, don't let us down." Whispered Bob, the giant poodle whined, then stood up and let out a bark. Then Bob mounted him like a cowboy out of the old west and set out on the mountain trail.

Chapter Four

By the time Bob had the alien ship in his sight it was beginning to get dark, what the heck was Erik doing down there, it looked like he was river dancing and he could just barely hear music, the words were saying something like "Lorrd have mercy on myy sssoul!" "Oh my god", the creature has driven him insane-thought Bob, it must be some kind of psychological torture to break Erik's will. Just as Bob came galloping up to them the music stopped playing, "Time for truth ray or death ray my friend" said the Lizard man, Bob aimed carefully as he rode up and fired the wrist laser at the robot with the death ray, he recognized the scoring on it's chest from their last encounter, he hit it right in the face blowing off it's head, then aiming again this time at the other robot he zapped it's head off as well, the Lizard King sat up from the rock he was perched on and pointed at Bob, at that moment Erik dived down toward some rocks. Grabbing two baseball sized rocks he hurled one rock at the beast's outstretched hand that illicited a spark as it struck the Lizard's hand, and the other rock hit the creature square between the eyes knocking him over backwards with an expression of utter contempt and surprise on it's face. Bob motioned for Erik to jump on the back of the dog behind the saddle, "Hurry, get on Erik!" shouted Bob, Erik eagerly did as he was told, they galloped at lightning speed toward the mountain path. They made it to the village clearing at the foot of the mountain pass, "I was raped by Clarence Baker the Lizard King Bob, don't you dare say a word about it to the others!" growled Erik, "Don't worry, I'll be careful what I say" whispered Bob, the gang had started the camp fire, Judith was waiting near the camp fire, her eyes red from crying, they looked up and saw them riding into the camp, they stopped near the fire and Erik slid off the poodle, "Merry Christmas darling" said Erik to Judith as she put her arms around Erik. She saw the red mark on his forehead & saw him lose his balance as he turned his head to cough. "Bob, what happened to Erik?" asked Judith, Bob hopped off the poodle whispering in it's ear, "go to bed sparky", Bob cleared his throat avoiding Judith's eyes, "He was tortured, I stopped the Lizard King Clarence before he could kill him." Judith held Erik by the arm, "Lean on me honey, yeah that's it, c'mon sit here next to me on the bamboo bench, he staggered and they both plopped their rear ends on the bench. "I can't shake the feeling that the computer chip is somewhere on the temple grounds, we could ask the new oracle but the trash heap seems to be making mistakes, maybe it's the new location, I don't know." "Perhaps we should just search for it when we have the light" said Temlok, "My people are very afraid, but very grateful, this Erik is a very brave warrior, perhaps he will save us all in the end." Just then they heard thumping in the distance and heavy breathing coming out of the darkness, and an errie singing off key like a screeching "LLLORRD HAVE MERCYYY ON MYY SSSOULLL! HA HA HA HA!" came the horrible voice out of the darkness, the Dwarves were frightened, "It's a demon!" They cried.

Just then against the night sky where the twin moons lit up the clouds they saw a giant silhiuette, it was getting closer and closer, "Fee Fye Foe Fum, I smell an englishman whose really dumb!" screeched the voice, and then they saw the twenty foot giant fat lady, naked bouncing up and down as she ran toward the firelight in all the fat wrinkly glory of her lewdness. "Oh dear God it looks like a Giant Rosie O'conell from earth's past!!" yelled Mike.

"Dear God in heaven, Help us!" shouted Temlok, suddenly it started to snow, the Golden statue of the Chumba Wumba holding the star creaked and groaned and then moved off it's base near the temple entrance and set down the star next to the fire, the statue was a good sixty feet tall, the fat lady only twenty feet so, "Look" said Judith, Father Christmas has performed another miracle, that giant statue that looks like Don Trumpster wearing speedos has come to protect us!" The giant Golden statue grabbed the naked fat lady, picked her up and whispered in her ear, "Your fired", and carried her over to the great trash heap and then fed the fat lady to the great trash heap, and said "It's over". Then the statue stepped back on to it's pedestal and struck a pose looking up toward the stars like a well oiled muscular greek god, and then moved no more. Suddenly a green light on the bottom of the Star setting next to the fire began beeping. Bob walked up to it, and pulled out a large computer chip encased in plastic, "The Lost Star Map, I've found the computer Chip!" Shouted Bob!! "Judith, run that chip back to Green on the ship" said Erik. "Yes, darling, don't worry Bob, I can take it from here." Bob gave Judith the chip, and she scurried off to the Quack and told Green all about it. "This calls for a celebration!" shouted Temlok, "Squirrel jerky and Acorn tea for everybody!"

Right about then they all heard growling, and hissing coming from the darkness, "SSSSSo you've defeated my cloned warrior, no matter we will have a showdown, I'll get you my pretty and your little dog too!" Shouted the Lizard King. " Have no fear, The Astral Beamer is here, and I will accept this challenge, c'mon Man Dragon meet me at the edge of town near the old abandoned well if you have the nads for it!" Shouted Bob. Bob walked toward the end of the vilage near the corn forrest toward the old well, " Come Coward and follow me if you dare!"

The twin moon light illuminated the beast as it followed Bob from out of the dark shadows, it hissed and growled! They stood a small distance from the well, like ancient gunfighters ready for death.

"You know I'm better than you Mr. Smiley face, why don't you put away your laser and prove me wrong, or is it perhaps that you are the coward?" asked the beast. "Clarence, or what ever your real name is, I might just take you up on that if you have the courage to only use fisticuffs!" replied Bob.

Bob's com link was beeping but he ignored it, "Alright little man, but surely you realize I'm ten times your weight class" said the Lizard King.

Bob took off his Wrist com/laser and tucked it in his back pocket, "There now, c'mon Lizard, let's see what you're made of!" said Bob the Astral beamer, the Lizard man charged, Bob used his invisible leg stretched out to trip the Lizard king. "Damn invisible legs, If I get my hands on you I swear I will break them, right before I make you into an omlet!" growled the beast, the beast lunged at Bob, and Bob landed a lucky right jab to it's kidney, The Lizard King laughed and swatted Bob in the face breaking and bloodying his nose. Bob staggered back toward the well, the Lizard landed another blow to Bob's face splitting his lower lip, Bob spit blood on the ground. "I know what you did to my friend, and I'm not walking away without giving you a royal beating villain, how dare you take the name of an angel as your own you piece of filth!" Hissed Bob right before he spit more blood on the ground. "I crap on your Christian mythologies, and that's all you are really, you're about to pass on to the world of myths forever Smiley face!" grunted the Lizard monster. "Bring it on Shith boy, or are all you Cylom lizards all talk and no action? Maybe that's why your kind became extinct and was replaced by a race of robots, that's why your race was written out of the never ending story because you're so lame!" replied Bob as he danced from side to side like a boxer, "Shut up little obsolete Hippy anachronism while I break your face in two" shouted the Lizard King as he landed a left cross to Bob's left eye, Bob staggered backwards and fell on his back in pain. The Lizard King smiled and giggled with Delight, "now with one lightning bolt I will at last eliminate the only threat here capable of stopping me, you're about to become toast little man!"shouted the Lizard King.

Suddenly a loud Whazzzzapp! Was heard hitting the huge Lizard Monster in the back of the head, the Cylom Lizard put his hand to the back of his head feeling a sticky wetness, and looked at his hand stained with his own blood, and then fell forward fainting on the ground a few feet away from where Bob lay gasping for breath. Standing there in the dark with a phaser rifle in one hand was Green the sweet candy girl, "Nobody messes with my man dirt bag, you just messed with the wrong boyfriend

Because now I'm pissed off, I'm not just going to hurt you, I'M GOING TO KILL YOU!!" growled Green as she walked up to the unconscious Lizard. She pointed the Phaser rifle point blank at his bloody head and squeezed off two more shots, VVVZZZAP, BVVZZZAP!! Tossing down the rifle she then picked up the Lizard and hoisted him up on her shoulders, and dragged him to the well, "You had this coming you son of a bitch, now enjoy your ill gotten gain, you deserve it toad!" said Green as she picked him up above her head with both hands, suddenly he twitched and electricity arced out of his hands frying Green's shell, she screamed and tossed him in. Then she fell back on the ground, and crawled to Bob, "It's okay baby, I'm here for you, I'll never leave you again, Robert speak to me please!" Bob whispered "Zu Zu's pettles…." "What Bob, I don't understand, what are you trying to tell me?" "Marry me" whispered Bob, "Yes darling, I will Marry you", she wept as she held him in her arms, touching a switch on her belt the song "I am woman" began playing by Helen Reddy. Meanwhile Erik went up to Mike and put his hand on his shoulder, "I know what has to be done now, I need a favor pal, go to the ship and fetch me a flash light, don't tell anyone what you're doing, just go, okay?" said Erik, "Okay buddy, I'll be right back."said Mike, and he quietly slipped away during Green's song and went to get the flash light, returned with it in hand, and handed it over to Erik who then walked toward the Mountain pass, Mike spoke up- "Erik, are you sure?" "I wouldn't be much of a hero if I wasn't, trust me I'm still hopped up on that super sauce, go help Green and Bob." With that Erik disapeared into the night as he followed the mountain trail back to the Cylom space craft. With Flash light on and the Super sauce working overtime keeping him awake Erik finally came to the alien space craft, looking down he found what he came for, the key cartridge to open the space craft! Picking it up he inserted it into the slot, the door opened, he went aboard and found no one, not even a robot. Then he came out of the ship, and closed the door and stuck the key in his pocket, and started back down the mountain trail toward camp. As he walked back into camp he overheard festivities going on strong as dwarves played little bongos and played chimes to an Old Geicko tune, "Every where I go, there's always something to remind me, of another place and time….", and it droned on and on, it had a soothing quality to it. Erik walked right up to the chief and handed him the key, "This is both your key to survival and wealth, for it will open the stars up to you; it is the key to the Cylom flagship, you and your people now no longer need to remain on this planet, you are free to roam the Cosmos!" volunteered Erik. "Again Erik, you prove yourself to be a hero", said Temlok, "I, er-we are grateful." So then he walked up to Mike, "Hi pal, I finally learned what both Bob and I needed pounding into our skulls, that to be a hero, you should never go off half cocked!!" said Erik.

"Real heroes get onto the Internet to donate money, like those web sites NationalCasa.Org, Wish.org, and Unicef.org, or like you know those TV phone lines to feed the children, we're just guys having adventures, not costumed crusaders, real heroes help people when those people need it the most, and that's a very rare quality indeed." Said Erik. Bob sat next to Green and moaned, "My faish is killing me!" moaned Bob. Erik went up to him and whistled, "Wow, that's quite a shiner you got there, but I gotta take my hat off to Green, Man woman where'd you learn to fight like that, you're a little toasty around the edges." Remarked Erik, "Yeah, but I did it for Bob because he's my pooky bear and I love him, now that A-hole is toast, and we can go home!" replied Green. Two Dwarven priests walked up to them and commented, "Thanks to the sacred scrolls of the Mahktar, we will be able to understand the technology of our slain enemy and control his star ship, so you are more than welcome to the device from the sacred statue."

Bob groaned, "well that fat lady has sung and if you don't mind the pun all's well, that ends well guys, just one last thing to do before we go back to the ship to get some shut eye". Said an achy Bob, "What's that?" said Mike, Bob flipped a switch on his belt and the song "I get by with a little help from my friends" began to play. Judith laughed, "It must be nice to have your own private stereo in your underwear, Honey come along I want to go keep Mina company in the ship before we turn in and drink hot cocoa with miniture marshmellows." She said, "Yes dear." Said Erik. The gang all headed for the ship, "Hey Winnie, why don't you come join us for some cocoa, we could use the company." Yelled Judith, Winnie then came running up to them, "I'd really love that, okay." They walked up to the ship in the middle of the corn field with Erik's flash light showing the way, and into the ship they went.

After they were all settled in the women were all drinking hot cocoa, and Winnie said, "By the way did I mention my boss is a vampire with a soul?"

"Really? Is he mean to you?" asked Mina. "No, he's the greatest boss in the world, since he has a soul he has a conscience, he's really a sweet pussycat deep down inside, I miss him, he was always consulting the powers that be, sort of like angels I suppose, which is funny because that's what I called him, Angel; before I died" replied Winny. "Oh, I'm sorry girls but I have to go use the little girl's room" said Mina, "Oh poo, don't worry sweety we won't run away" said Green. "Say, Irene, are you feeling alright you look like those burns hurt, do you want some ointment?" asked Judith, "No, I'm fine thanks, I'll be okay as soon as I join Bob in the bedroom, I just need a good night's sleep." Replied Green. Meanwhile in the lavoratory, Mina squeezes out a turd and stands up to wipe, when she turns to look at it, she is shocked to see it resembles Carmen Daly from Muse-TV, suddenly it spoke to her, "That's the way you do it, your money for nothin, and your chits for free", said the turd, she tossed in the toilet paper she wiped with and flushed the toilet, then it said as it went down "Eat my candy Coney" "Gurgle gurgle" whoosh went the toilet water and it was gone. "Maybe it's an omen, wait till I tell the girls a turd that looked and sounded like Carmen Daly spoke to me, maybe it means my baby will be a rock star!" Mina thought out loud.

Chapter Five

The morning sun blazed above the horizon, life began to stir within the Star ship Quack, Winnie was the first to get up and use the rest room, she then walked onto the main bridge & sat at Navigation control waiting for Green.

Green came on board the bridge with a sleeping Bob in her arms, "Shshsh, we'll wait for him to wake," said Irene Green. Eventually Mina and Judith came on board and sat at the con, Mike manned both communications and Security, Green manned the science station, Erik stayed in the engine room monitoring energy levels. "Six thirty AM, ready for launch and orbital

insertion Green", said Winnie, "Mina charge the Ion nacelles to 70%, Bob honey wake up it's time to go." Said Green. Bob woke up, Winnie said, "Well boss, it's future earth or bust, time for earth was different than your time because of time dialation, it won't be the earth that you knew but it's still home." "Launch, and all ahead full" said Bob. The ship slowly rose up off the ground, rapidly gaining speed at a 45 degree angle, eventually it reached orbit, then shot upward past the twin moons, and into the depths of space heading for earth. Time slowed to a crawl, the ship warped its way into the Solar neighborhood within the orbit of Xena's planet aimed at a Jovian partial injection, eventually slingshotting towards earth. The sun was dangerously large, Mercury was swallowed by the corona, and Venus flew just above the solar flares coming from an orange sun. They dipped below earth's Ionisphere entering in a zig zag pattern like a descending cork screw toward Los Angeles. The ship gently settled down in the middle of a city intersection with a light thump. "Well, I'm home" said Winnie, "All I have to do is find Wolfram and hart law firm to use their books on magic for a time travel spell, I will be okay so nobody worry." With that Winnie stood up and headed for the door, "Winnie" said Bob, She stopped, "I know I speak for us all when I say Good Luck, we'll keep tabs on you in case you need us." "Thanks" she said, and left, eventually the outer door opened and Winnie stepped out into the hot windy intersection in down town Los Angeles, the streets and everything was deserted. Bravely she walked on down the deserted street and didn't look back even once. The ship door closed, and the ship gently rose off the street and flew into the sky heading due East, and then northeast to Great Britain, or rather, what was left of it. A few minutes later, sixty yards down the street in the direction Winnie was walking in, a flash of light and suddenly a phone booth appeared in the middle of the street.

The closer she got to the phone booth, the more it seemed like two bearded men were in it opening the door of the booth, she quickened her pace. Finally she reached the phone booth, it couldn't be a hallucination could it? Thought Winnie, suddenly the dark haired hippy spoke to her, "Salutations Most excellent lady fair we are Phil and Fred, and together we are" They both said simultaneously "Wild Horsies", "Most excellent hostess" went on the blond haired hippy, "We are doing research for a book, would you be so gracious as to come with us back to the twenty-first century and help answer some questions about future earth?" "I'd love to" said Winnie smiling, she joined them in the phone booth and they both said "Excellent and most triumphant"! With that the phone booth door shut and the dark haired lad punched a few numbers of the phone and the phone booth vanished in flash of light whisking all three of them back to the year 2007 C.E., and as for our friends in the starship landing in Great Britain on a country estate, they had reached their destination. "Well", said Bob, "This is it, sensors have located the time portal that leads back to your world, and as it just turns out this is the Kotter Estate once owned by the famous Harry Kotter, this is where we part company. We'll fly by Los Angeles for a sensor sweep to check on

Winnie's progress, and then we will leave the solar system to find an inhabited world where Green and I can be legally married."

Mike said, "Thanks Bob, you've really made a difference in our lives".

Bob said, "Good luck gang, it will be okay."

With that Mike, Mina, Erik, and Judith disembarked the ship, and entered the old Victorian mansion. Then Bob popped a tape cassette in and hit play,

Gary Wright's Dream weaver started up, and the ship lifted off the ground and flew away. Meanwhile, The gang walked into the foyer and up a flight of stairs, finally stopping at the top landing at the attic door, they opened the door and walked in. toward the end of the dimly lit room was an old man in a black robe with a long white beard sitting in a rocking chair next to an inn table with a crystal ball on it. Next to the crystal ball was a closed black journal with a wand lying on top of it. To his left was an old full length mirror, to his right two love seats sat facing the mirror. On the old man's face were round spectacles, he looked up and noticed them coming into the room, "Welcome, I've been waiting a very long time for you, come in and have a seat", said the old man. "You've been expecting us?"asked Mike.

"Yesss, yes, but let me introduce myself, I am Sir Harry Kotter, Wizard extrordinaire, an alumni of Hogfart's school of witchcraft and wizardry." Rambled the old Wizard. The gang came in and sat down in the love seats, "You must be very old", said Erik. At that the wizard laughed, " or very dead, you see I am but a sliver of mine own soul, a shade existing as a horcrush, solid only in this place and time, and time is running short." Said the old wizard. "Can you help us get home?" asked Mina. "I'm sure I can, but the question is can you handle going home?" said the wizard.

Erik interrupted them, "Wait a minute, why couldn't we stay here?"

"Because young man, in case you have not noticed, everyone on earth fled into space ages ago, this is a world about to die as the sun turns into a red gas giant and swallows the earth as the sun expands, which should be very soon now I think." Replied the wizard. Everyone in the gang shouted, "Winnie!!" "Oh, I know what you're thinking, you're concerned about your lady friend, but my crystal ball tells me she hitched a ride back into the past with two time travelers, soon it will be your turn to go back in time to your own reality, your own earth, courtesy of the magic mirror given to me as a gift by the wizard wyatt, goodness, I haven't thought of the charm ones in years, how time does fly by." Replied the wizard as he stroked his white beard with his hand absent mindedly, his white flowing hair reached down to his shoulders. "Well, what are we waiting on, I don't want to be burned up by the sun old man!" exclaimed Judith, "Harry, please call me Harry, I'm sorry but I have to give you proper instructions and clues, your destinies are intertwined, and Mina's child will grow up to be a White lighter, a champion of good with great powers, please see to it The Wizard Paul stays out of trouble, you've met his future self but the Paul you will meet is the founder of Magic school and if it wasn't for those damn avatars everything would be fine!" rambled on the Wizard. Mike interjected, "You mean, we get to meet that guy when he's alive, and he really is a wizard?" "I told you already it's up to Mina's son to do what must be done, The wizard Paul creates a horcrush of himself, and if you get in trouble you must find it, it will be in a journal, it will be in the possession of an actress that he is fond of, but beware, reversing time is dangerous. I should have listened to that house elf….." said Harry. Erik said in a puzzled fashion, "Why, what do elves have to do with it?" "Oh it's just dejavu, remember to stay away from Adam Warlock, he becomes the leader of the avatars, his code name is King James, it's a biblical reference, the egotistical bastard! I'm sorry but those are all the clues I'm allowed to give you." Said Harry, and with that he picked up his wand and said " this journal of mine that created this horcrush of me was the right thing to do, soon I will be going home too", he then pointed the wand at the mirror and said, "Kukucatchu!!" Suddenly the mirror glowed gold then white, and then an image of hippies and flower children filled the mirror and suddenly the gang was wearing hippie getups and the song California dreaming by the Mamas and the Pappas filled the room.

"Quickly now before the magic dies, you'll end up in Woodstock in the 60's, now go, go, jump into the mirror, what are you waiting on get out of here!"exclaimed the wizard Harry Kotter. They all jumped through one at a time, first Judith, then Mina, then Erik, then Mike, and then the mirror glowed green and red and cracked, then all was quiet and the light was gone. Shaking a bit the old man put down his wand on the inn table next to his journal and said "well, old boy it's done." Harry stood up and walked over to the cracked mirror, "Seven years of bad luck" he giggled, then he turned serious as the light in the room darkened and the sun turned red, he turned to look through the window behind his chair, a tear ran down his face. The red sun expanded and swallowed the earth and the cities and countrysides burst into flames as the seas boiled away, and then Harry Potter's world was gone.

Meanwhile back in Mike's world in the past at woodstock a bright flash occurred above an abandoned blanket and all the gang plopped out of thin air onto the blanket unharmed. Jimmy Hendrix was playing Purple haze "excuse me while I kiss the sky", the gang all hugged. Erik said, "Guys, it is a wonderful life."

Much later....2004 at Saint Mary's Catholic church.

In front of the Church after the doors have closed, The Raisins stop by. "Chet, are you sure Paul made it here, look man, we can't even get in now, they started church already!" shouted the two and a half inch raisin man to his raisin buddies. "Yeah, Page said he'd be here after his girlfriend Teresa dumped him Joe, its all over the grapevine man!" hollered back Chet. Joe the Raisin man put his cool shades on and said, " That's rough, but it gives me an idea. Hey Mikey, stick that old tape in the boom box, the one with heard it on the grapevine." "I know its here somewhere" said the Michael Jackson raisin, he pulls a tape cassette out of his duffle bag, sticks it in the boom box and hits play. The song I heard it on the grape vine begins to play and the two dozen raisin men begin to dance in front of the church to the song. Mean while inside the whole Powers that be gang are inside the church watching the Priest bless Paul, and the priest asks Paul what he would like the priest to bless him with and Paul says, "I would like a pure heart." Erik turns to Bob the yellow Smiley face alien and says, "I think everything is going to turn out alright." Bob the astral beamer replies, " You know old chap, I think you're right, as long as the Avatars are kept away, I think Spring is right around the corner." Bob then sticks his tape into his walkman to play California dreamin.

And they all lived happily ever after, Thee End.

Lightning Source UK Ltd.
Milton Keynes UK
UKHW05f1408200718
325960UK00009B/35/P